This book belongs to

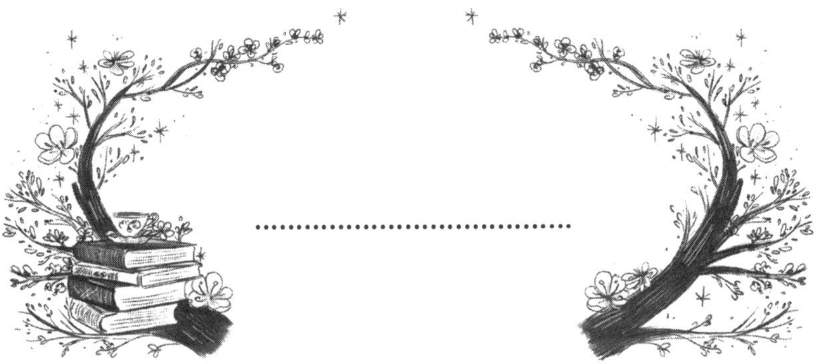

....

For Nan, for Laurel and Craig, for Leigh Klein,
who have all given me a home

The Ballad of Melodie Rose

Kate Gordon

UQP

1
Memories and forgotten things

Melodie Rose could remember, precisely, the moment she knew she was dead.

It happened as she stood, for the first time ever, on the steps of Direleafe Hall, her hand raised to knock, a hard stone step beneath her feet, the smell of cut grass and the sound of night-bird lullabies in the air.

A wooden door was before her, cut into a strange, grey, forbidding building, so tall she couldn't see the top of it.

She remembered her fingertips, pressed to the door, and how it seemed to vibrate, to *hum*. It felt as if she had been born in that moment.

Which was funny, if you knew the truth.

Melodie had a note pinned to her duffel coat. She had read it twice and both times it made no sense.

This here is my Melodie Rose. She belongs to Direleafe Hall now. I can't see her anymore. I can't see anything clearly. There is no sunrise. Please keep her safe here. Love her the way she deserves.

The note made no sense to Melodie because her mother had not said goodbye. It made no sense because she had not said when she would return. It made no sense because Melodie's head was full of moths, now. It was full of clouds and smudges and birdsong, and everything before this moment was *gone*.

There had been a break, a snap, an eclipse of the sun. Only the parts that began *here* were illuminated fully. Everything that came *before* was clouded entirely. Some small grubby-fingered pixie had made a mess of it all.

Memory is a funny thing, Melodie thought.

It was like a film reel, unspooling, some frames in focus and others not, and some of the images so fingerprint-smudged that it was hard to make them out at all.

When she closed her eyes tightly, Melodie could only see *flickers* of her life before Direleafe Hall. She turned them over in her palm, held them up to the light ...

★

Her mother's laughter, and then her tears.

Bare feet, walking away.

Her father's eyes, like Fred Astaire's.

A hand, holding hers and then falling.

Her heart breaking entirely.

★

The only frames completely in focus were a hundred facts about mountain goats and twenty facts about graves and thousands upon thousands of other curiosities about bats and bees and broken bones. She knew she had read all these things in books and that they had seemed so *important* to her. Now, they filled every nook and cranny of her. They squeezed out everything else.

Nothing made sense, everything was dark, and her coat was itching. And this place, Direleafe Hall, was so big, and she was so small and frightened.

And for some reason, someone had tipped out an inkwell over every part of the sky, blackening out the stars.

And for some reason, someone had broken her heart.

The door opened. It was bright inside. An old woman stood in the light. She looked right through Melodie. As if Melodie was not there.

Melodie stared at the old woman, unspeaking, which made no sense because Melodie *always* talked. Melodie *loved* to talk.

Didn't she?

Melodie scrunched up her face. She wasn't sure. She wasn't sure of *anything*. She felt as if she might float away.

The woman looked right past her, into the night.

Melodie thought of a song about night-time. A song from *before*. A song from memory. She tried to sing it, but no words would come and, instead, all that left her mouth was humming.

The old woman blinked. Once, twice, three times. 'Where did you come from?' she said.

And Melodie whispered, 'I can't remember.'

'I thought you might be a ghost,' the old woman said, her voice snagging as if on a hook, and then, after a pause, she added, 'I thought you might be my daughter.'

Melodie looked down at her fingertips and, in the all-encompassing darkness, they seemed to *disappear*.

2
Melodie is a ghost

I thought you might be a ghost ...

'If I am a ghost,' Melodie said to herself, 'then all of this makes sense.'

As to why the old woman could see Melodie, well ... Melodie did not know the answer to that. She knew so many things about fish and fir trees, and even fagus and fungus, but not so very much about ghosts. She could only guess that it had something to do with this place.

There was something very odd about Direleafe Hall. It had a *heartbeat.* It felt like a place where the dead might be seen.

A memory fluttered into focus.

★

A hand, holding hers.

Her father. Her father falling.

And so was she.

★

'Melodie Rose,' the old woman said, breaking her out of her dream. 'You are welcome here, at Direleafe Hall, in my school – my school for girls. You are welcome in my home. My name is Ms Gallow ...'

Hello, Ms Gallow! Melodie wished to cry. *I know thirteen facts about bats!*

She swallowed down the facts, though, all the way to her toes, and she curtseyed instead because curtseying was what people did when they met someone important. She remembered that from books.

'Pleased to meet you, Ms Gallow,' Melodie echoed, politely.

'Oh, no! Don't call me that.' The old women chuckled, her eyes twinkling like stars. She leaned close and said, 'You, my dear little Melodie Rose, you may call me *Grandma*.'

'Are you?' Melodie whispered. 'Are you my grandma?'

The woman's brow furrowed. 'You really don't remember?'

Melodie shook her head. 'I don't remember much of anything before this moment.'

The woman nodded, slowly, and she muttered, 'I've heard that can happen, when a heart breaks. Memory can sometimes ... falter.'

Melodie nodded. Because this made even *more* sense of it all. If memory falters when a heart breaks, it must disappear entirely when a person dies, when a heart itself is a thing of memory.

She looked up at her grandmother. 'My mother,' Melodie said, 'is your daughter?'

'That's right,' said Ms Gallow, peering into the darkness again.

'She left me,' said Melodie. She tore the note from her jacket and passed it to Ms Gallow.

Ms Gallow put it in her pocket. Still smiling, she extended her hand. 'Come,' she said. 'Let's go to the refectory. It's time for you to meet the other pupils. Classes don't start for a little while yet – we're still on holidays. But it will be nice, I think, for you to have this time. To acquaint yourself with Direleafe and make firm friends with the girls.'

'Why are the girls here?' Melodie asked. 'If it's holidays?'

Her grandmother looked sad for a moment. 'This is their home,' was all she said. She brightened. 'Come, now. I'll tell you who's who.'

'But why?' Melodie asked, boldly. 'And how? How can you introduce me if I am a ghost?'

Her grandmother laughed, as if she'd made a joke.

But she didn't say it wasn't true.

'Come,' she said to Melodie Rose.

And Melodie, her voice a shattered thing because she had just discovered that she was both *dead* and that she had a grandmother, replied, 'All right, Grandma.' And then she recovered her nerve just a little and added, 'Did you know that elephants can't jump?'

3
The other girls

Melodie stood at the door to the Direleafe Hall refectory. It was so bright in there, after all the darkness outside, and she saw that the room was filled with candles. Outside, it all seemed so grim, but in here ... in here, it was still run-down and *old*, but the candlelight and the laughter made it all feel so ...

Alive.

The room was mostly empty. When her grandmother had spoken of *the girls*, Melodie had pictured a school teeming with children, like fish in a tank. Instead, there was only a handful, and only two who looked her age.

One was tiny, her hair as pale as snow. 'That is Rowan,' Ms Gallow said, smiling fondly. 'She is in your year. And somewhere around here should be—'

There was a crash from somewhere just outside the refectory, and a dark-haired, dark-eyed girl darted past, a roast chicken leg in her hand.

'Ines Amontillado!' Ms Gallow muttered – not angry but despairing – and marched off in the direction of the fleeing child.

Melodie was left alone.

None of the girls looked her way.

She was invisible.

'They don't see me,' she whispered.

And Melodie found that, curiously, perhaps it was all right. Perhaps she did not want to be seen. Being seen felt ...

Dangerous.

And, anyhow, it seemed *impossible*, too, because she was a ghost.

'They don't see us either,' a voice behind

her said. 'We've become accustomed to it.'

Melodie turned, back towards the corridor. Three girls stood there, in a row.

One of them smiled at her, bashfully.

One of them peered at her, as if she were a specimen.

The last one – the speaking one, a tiny imp-like girl – made daggers with her eyes. She was the one who beckoned to Melodie.

Melodie followed her into the hallway.

'There used to be more,' the glowering one said. 'More girls at Direleafe Hall. Not anymore. That's why the Lady in White wants to flatten it.'

'The *who*?' Melodie whispered.

The girl appeared not to hear her. 'None of *them* are like us.' She gestured at the handful of girls in the refectory, who laughed and sang and ate great piles of potatoes. 'They come and they go, and we forget most of them, in time. Living girls are so *fleeting*.'

She turned to Melodie. '*You* are like us,' she said. 'Aren't you? You must be if you can see us.

Only the dead can see us. Only the dead can't be seen.'

Melodie nodded.

'Are you frightened?' said the shy one. 'You look a bit frightened. You don't need to be. What harm can we do?'

'Speak for yourself,' said the glowering one. 'I'm joking. Sort of,' she said to Melodie. 'But you really don't need to be scared of us. You're one of us. And if you're here, you're stuck here, so you're stuck with *us*, I'm afraid.'

'What do you mean?' asked Melodie. 'What do you mean, *stuck here*?'

'You must have died here,' the girl explained, plainly. 'So, you're stuck here forever.'

'Unless—' the shy girl began.

'Hush, Lucy,' said the glowering one.

'Stuck here,' Melodie murmured. 'Stuck with you ...' She looked up at the three girls. 'You're not going anywhere?' she asked.

She thought of her mother, and her tears, and her bare feet, *leaving her*. She thought of her father's hand, slipping away.

The one who seemed to be watching Melodie with a scientist's eyes said, matter-of-factly, 'In life, we three weren't friends at all, but death binds you to a place and to people. And, look, if we can accept each other in all our weirdness—'

'Speak for yourself,' the glaring girl repeated.

'—then we will *always* accept you.'

'Always,' repeated Lucy, softly. 'Please, don't be afraid of us. You're not, are you?'

Melodie shook her head. And she found it was true. After all, she was a ghost, too.

And, curiously, she was not afraid of being *seen* by these ghost girls either. If it were true that they were stuck together, and they would like her no matter what ... perhaps being seen by them would be all right.

The scientist asked, curiously, 'So, how *did* you come to die at Direleafe Hall?'

'We've never seen you here before,' the grumpy girl said, folding her arms.

And Melodie could only shake her head. 'I can't remember,' she said.

The timid one gave a little sigh. 'What a blessing.'

'Don't you remember *anything*?' the scientist persisted.

Melodie thought, again, of her father's hand and how they had both collapsed. 'I remember falling, out on the street, near my home. I thought, perhaps, I never stood up ...'

The glaring girl shook her head. 'That can't be the case,' she said. 'You can't have died *there*. Like we said, when you die, you stay in that place if your soul is tethered there. If you don't go—'

'On,' the shy one interrupted, sadly.

'You must have died here,' said the scientist. 'You must have died *tonight*. Perhaps your mother brought you here to die.'

'You saw her?' Melodie asked.

The girls nodded.

'She looked familiar,' said the scientist. She

shrugged. 'But all living girls seem familiar. We've seen so many in our time – they all look the same.'

'She wore no shoes,' said the gentle one. 'And she was crying.'

'She was crying because ... I died,' Melodie whispered. 'But why would she bring me here to die? It doesn't make sense. Except ...' She gasped. 'Ms Gallow is my grandmother. This place ...'

'It's your true home,' said the shy one, smiling. 'It does make sense.'

Melodie nodded. 'It does ...' A memory, sudden, made her fingertips tingle. 'My mother believed in ghosts,' she said. 'She believed in *everything*. She would have known about the *sticking* thing. She wanted me to stay here forever.'

'Enough of this chatter,' the glaring girl said. 'We don't even know your name yet.'

Melodie smiled. She smiled because *everything* made sense, now.

'My name,' she said, 'is Melodie Rose.'

'Welcome,' said Lucy. 'You belong here, now. You belong to *us*. You belong here at Direleafe Hall.'

Melodie smiled wider, then. Brighter than the sun.

As bright as the Melodie Rose she felt she was inside.

4

Florence, Lucy and Nell

Their names were Florence, Lucy, and Nell.

Florence was the scientist. She had eyes like a summer storm and hair as white as goose down. She was smart as shoe polish and mostly *brain*, but her heart was as big as mountains, too.

Lucy was the shy, quiet one. She had umber-brown skin and corkscrew curls. She was timid, unsure and sad, and exceptionally kind.

Nell was the one who always spoke first, who glowered and growled and stomped. She was as small as a mouse but louder and bolder than the other two combined, and sometimes her tongue was acid.

They were, all of them, *wonderful*, to Melodie Rose.

'Thank you for your welcome,' said Melodie. And she smiled, despite herself. And then, because she *could*, she blurted, 'Did you know that flamingos are naturally white? It's their diet that turns them pink.'

'You know a lot,' said Nell.

Melodie shook her head. 'Only about some things.'

Nell grinned wickedly in return. 'A girl who knows things could be extremely useful to us,' she said. And then, 'Ms Gallow's coming back. We'll see you soon, Melodie Rose.' Nell considered Melodie a moment longer. 'Probably best not to tell your grandmother about us. Or that you are a ghost.'

Lucy nodded. 'She might love you less,' she sighed, 'if she knew.'

Nell took the hands of the other two girls, and the three of them disappeared.

Ms Gallow returned to Melodie's side. 'Did I hear you speaking, Melodie? Who is there?'

'Nobody and nothing, Grandma,' said Melodie. 'Only cobwebs and dust.'

And the old woman smiled, and her dark eyes rolled, and she said, 'Oh, yes. Well. Dust and cobwebs. Cobwebs and dust. There is much of both here at Direleafe Hall. Now, I have the small matter to solve of Ines Amontillado ...' Ms Gallow gestured towards a black-haired, brown-skinned, glaring girl, with chicken grease on her face. Ms Gallow sighed. 'In the meantime, would you like to stay here and have some dinner, Melodie Rose, or go to my cottage and sleep? You look tired.'

'I am tired. I think I'd like to go to the cottage, please,' said Melodie.

'Wait here, Ines,' Ms Gallow said, firmly.

Ines continued her scowling.

And then Ms Gallow led Melodie out of the hall and over the grass and to the front door of her cottage.

On the way, Melodie looked up at the sky. She could still see no stars. But then she saw the faintest one, half-hiding behind a cloud. And then it bobbed down and away.

'I see you,' Melodie whispered.

Inside the cottage it was dusty. There were cracks in the walls like sorrows. But it was cosy. And it was friendly in a haphazard sort of way. There were bookshelves, everywhere. One of them only had books about animals. Books about animal facts. Melodie ran her fingertip across the crackled spines.

'Here is your home,' Ms Gallow said, simply, as Melodie gazed around. 'You can be here ...' She looked askance at her granddaughter. 'In whichever way you choose. Exactly as you are,' she finished. Then she clapped her hands and said, 'Light a candle, won't you? This place is so dim once the sun has gone down, and I'm trying to save on the electrics bill.' Her smile drooped. 'On *all* the bills,' she muttered.

As Ms Gallow left, Melodie looked around. She walked to the kitchen window and stared out, back at Direleafe Hall. It was so tall, so imposing, so *grand*, in the night-time and from further away. It was only up close that you saw the cracks in the grey façade; that you realised it was flawed and vulnerable, just like the rest of us. It was only up close that you could feel its heartbeat.

The ghost girls were right.

She belonged to this place. She belonged *here*.

She took a match, then, and she lit a candle, and the whole room echoed with light.

5
Discoveries

The following evening, the four ghost girls sat at the gates of Direleafe Hall together. They watched the sheep, who rested in the fields beyond. They watched the circling night-birds and the scampering rabbits and all that life *outside*.

Behind them, in Direleafe Hall, Ms Gallow was preparing dinner for the girls. Ines Amontillado was 'helping' as punishment.

Melodie Rose was supposed to be getting to know the other pupils. But that was impossible, of course, so instead she was getting to know the other ghosts like her.

And she was getting to know all about Direleafe.

'So, what do you think of our hall?' said Lucy, smiling up at Melodie. 'Isn't it lovely?'

'It's a wreck,' Florence said, not unkindly, only matter-of-factly. Florence said everything that way. 'It's all worn down and almost broken.'

'The Lady in White says it's broken *already*,' Nell said, 'so what does it matter if it's broken more?'

'Who *is* the Lady in White?' Melodie asked Nell. 'You talked about her last night. That's not her *real* name, is it?'

Nell rolled her eyes. 'Obviously not.'

'We don't know what her real name is,' said Lucy.

'We only know that she is desperately trying to buy Direleafe,' said Florence.

Nell crossed her arms. '*I* found that out,' she said, smugly.

'Why?' Melodie asked. *She can't*, is what she didn't say. *Because I only just got here. Because*

I died here. Because I can't remember anything before here, so here is all that exists.

Nell lifted a shoulder. 'I told you last night. There are hardly any pupils here, not anymore, the electrics are faulty, the water is brown and all anyone has to eat are potatoes ...'

Lucy continued, sadly, 'And the Lady in White sees all that and thinks it's broken and old and worthless and about how she could turn the land into a fancy *resort*.'

Nell leaned in. 'I found out that this means a place for rich people to go and have *baths*.' Nell's nose wrinkled with disgust. She waved a hand. 'She's been hassling Ms Gallow for years, though it took me a long time to know that's what it was. I've been watching her, every time she comes, walking up that path—'

'And never *once* looking at the rabbits,' interrupted Florence. 'Or the Tunbridge buttercups.'

'At first it was, perhaps, every year she came and, lately, every month,' said Nell. 'Ms Gallow keeps letting her in, for who-knows-why, and all the other times the Lady in White left scowling but last time she smiled like a *witch*. She knows she's breaking Ms Gallow down.'

'She's going to crush Direleafe,' said Florence. She clapped one hand on top of the other. 'Like a flower field flattened by a storm.'

'She's going to crumble it into pieces,' whispered Lucy, rubbing at her eyes.

'It is our home,' they said as one.

'It's got all our histories in it,' Florence said. 'If they crumble it to pieces, the histories of us will be gone and so will we. A person can't survive if their stories are gone. It's science.'

Melodie felt her lip tremble. 'It might be a bit broken but that doesn't make it worthless. And old doesn't mean bad. The Pyramids are old and so is the Taj Mahal. I've seen them in books. They're wonderful.'

'People visit the Pyramids,' Lucy said. 'Almost nobody sends their children here anymore.'

'It's a new world,' Nell said. 'When I was a pupil here, Direleafe Hall was the only school for miles, and parents sent their girls here – and once, even a *boy* – from all over the island. Now, they want their children to go to fancy schools in the city, not damp, falling-down ones in the middle of windswept moors, no matter how happy the children are here. Parents these days, I've come to believe, are less concerned with whether their children are happy and more with that they are *seen* to be happy. They don't believe a child can be happy in a place that isn't shiny, in a place that's full of dust, and—'

'How do we fix it?' Melodie interrupted.

'You only just came here,' Florence said. 'Why do you want to fix it at all?'

'*We* can't fix it,' said Nell, looking at Florence and Lucy. 'We can't do anything. We don't know enough about the world in this century to have any clue what to do.' She peered at Melodie. 'But you know things. And

Ms Gallow sees you. That's strange, now that I come to think of it.'

'But not unprecedented,' said Florence. 'Remember Mabel Clattersham? She saw Wonder. And Wonder never saw us at all. This *seeing* thing seems to me like very flimsy science.'

'I suppose it's because Ms Gallow's my family,' Melodie said. 'And my mother said I belong here and when she comes back, well ...' Her arms prickled, and she felt a kind of glowing inside at the thought of her mother returning. The glowing turned to cinders when she thought of her mother returning to a place where she *was not*, a place that *was no longer*. She shook her head. 'But, Nell, I don't know things. I don't *remember* anything. I only know useless information about mice and manta rays.'

'Still,' said Nell, 'there's something about you, Melodie Rose. Something ...' She rolled her eyes. 'I don't know, *special*, I suppose.'

‘Whatever it is, it’s not enough to save Direleafe Hall. Not by myself,’ said Melodie.

‘Well,’ Nell said, ‘there is always Hollowbeak.’

‘Who is Hollowbeak?’ Melodie asked.

Florence shrugged. ‘We don’t know, really. We only know that he’s a bird, of the family Corvidae.’

‘We know he is grouchy,’ said Lucy, shuddering. ‘And a little bit frightening.’

‘We know more than that,’ said Nell, but when everyone turned to her, she raised a shoulder. ‘At least ... I think I *once* knew more about him but it’s only that ... I’ve forgotten.’ She shook her head. ‘Memory is a funny thing,’ she said. ‘When you’re a ghost it becomes even stranger.’

‘What does he look like?’ asked Melodie.

‘He is small and black and button-eyed,’ Nell replied. ‘And he is part of Direleafe Hall. As much as the dusty windows and the mildewed walls and your grandmother. Hollowbeak is always here, apart from that little while, when he disappeared. But he's back now.'

'And how will I find him?' asked Melodie Rose.

Lucy leaned close, and she whispered, 'Look towards the stars. Sitting on the closest thing to them – that is where Hollowbeak will be.'

6
Hollowbeak

Hollowbeak sat on the roof of Direleafe Hall. His claws curled around a shingle, holding tight. His feathers ruffled in the midnight breeze, and he bathed in the moonlight.

He was ... *returned*.

He had thought he might go, to the next place, to the stars. He was turned away.

You are not for this place, Hollowbeak Crow. You belong at Direleafe Hall.

Hollowbeak had no choice but to fly ...

down ...

down ...

down ...

When he'd landed, back again, on the roof of Direleafe Hall, he'd expected things to be the same as when he'd left. The same season. The same sky.

And the girls – he thought he would recognise the girls. Wonder and Mabel were gone, of course, but the rest of them ...

Amelia would be there. And Eloise.

Georgiana Kinch.

There would be newlings, naturally, in first form, but most of them he would know.

Except ...

Except, he didn't. Instead of so many girls streaming through the gates like fish swimming into the belly of a whale, there were only scattered clutches of girls – and he knew none of them.

They were *all* newlings. Every one.

Their uniforms were different – shorter skirts and jumpers in place of cardigans. The hairstyles were different, too. Some of the girls even wore it *short*.

Something had changed.

The whole world, it seemed, had shifted. As if Direleafe Hall were a steam train – as if it were now at the next station on.

It was on his third day back at Direleafe Hall that Hollowbeak finally spied a familiar face. She stood on the doorstep, instructing the pupils in some kind of game with rattan balls and sticks.

It took him this long to know her because she had changed so much.

Her black hair was dappled with white, now. Her proud jaw was slackened, and there were nooks beneath her eyes. There were lines by her lips and on her brow that were not there before.

Before.

Before, when she was Ms Gallow, Wonder's teacher. She had been young, then, and strong.

Now, she was older. Now, she was weary.

And it was only when Hollowbeak saw this, *knew* this – knew *her* – that he realised.

Somehow, while he was in the sky, in the stars, a hole had appeared in time and he had fallen through it, and it was later, now.

And Ms Gallow was whittled down. And Direleafe Hall was crumbling. And there were so very few girls.

He closed his eyes, and he saw Wonder as she walked away from him, away to the stars. She looked over her shoulder and smiled, and she said to him, 'Look after Direleafe Hall, Hollowbeak. Look after Ms Gallow. Look after the girls. And let them look after you.'

He could hear them, almost, now. Wonder's words, echoing down from the stars.

Look after Direleafe Hall ...

But what could one measly crow do for a crumbling old school?

One warm summer night, though, as he bathed beneath the moon, in his favourite silver birch tree, a girl came and sat down beside him.

'Hello, Hollowbeak,' she said.

Her name was Melodie.

7
Hollowbeak and Melodie Rose

'Melodie *Rose*,' she told Hollowbeak when he asked her. And then she went on. 'Did you know roses have been cultivated for five thousand years and that *spiders* can make them die? Because of the bees. Roses need bees and spiders *eat them*.'

I … did not know that, said Hollowbeak. He narrowed his eyes at this strange, talkative girl. *Where did you come from?* he asked.

Melodie smiled. 'I lived for twelve years somewhere else entirely, or maybe more than one place. I don't remember. And now I am *here*.'

You don't remember?

The girl faltered; her face flickered. 'No. Not most of it. I don't know why. I suppose I lost it all when I died, when I became a ...' She waved a hand around herself. '*Ghost.*' The smile reignited. 'Now, though, I am at Direleafe Hall, in a tree, with *you*, Hollowbeak.'

What do you want from me? he asked.

He was grouchy at the unwelcome appearance of this unexpected girl. This new girl seemed just a bit *much*. With curls as red as fox fur, freckles like sparks and eyes like a midsummer sky, this new girl was tall and sturdy and seemed to have *too many bones*.

There was too much of her, entirely.

And now, it seemed, she was *humming*.

Hollowbeak let it continue for as long as his old nerves could take it. And then his nerves yelled, *No!* and his beak cried, *Stop!*

Melodie startled. And then she smiled. 'Oh. Was I doing it again?'

If by 'doing it', you mean humming like an angry cicada, then, yes, Hollowbeak grumbled.

‘Cicadas don’t hum. They *sing*,’ said Melodie. Her face scrunched. ‘I think I used to sing,’ she whispered. And then she began humming again.

Hollowbeak sighed and stifled a growl. *What do you want, Melodie Rose?*

Melodie crossed her fingers for luck and held them out so Hollowbeak could see. 'I want you to help me save Direleafe Hall. Please?' she added, politely. She smiled, and it was as if the sun had emerged from a cloak of clouds.

And it made a memory, in Hollowbeak's mind, of the first time Wonder had smiled at him. And the last time she had smiled, over her shoulder, before she walked into the stars.

Look after Direleafe Hall, Hollowbeak ...

It was almost as if he heard her voice, singing from the sky.

Hollowbeak's feathers ruffled. He wanted to help, of course. He wanted to keep his promise to Wonder. But who was this girl, this new girl? Why was she asking *him*? And would she – Hollowbeak cursed himself for even thinking it – would she break his heart, like Wonder had?

How do you think I might help save Direleafe Hall? Hollowbeak asked Melodie Rose. *I'm only a bird.*

Melodie inclined her head. 'I know some things about crows, Hollowbeak.'

Hollowbeak cleared his throat.

Before he could say a thing more, Melodie continued, her words falling out like water from a tap. 'I know that crows are extremely clever. They solve problems and mysteries. I know, also, that crows can tell if a person is mean. They know how to spot a *villain*. I know, Hollowbeak, that crows are mostly solitary, but they don't like to be alone always. They like to have friends and a home. They will protect their friends and their home 'til the end of all things.'

Hollowbeak opened his beak to reply, but Melodie barrelled on. 'We'd make a good team. If you're not yet convinced, I can also provide songs – hummed, not sung. It seems I *can't* sing. And facts. And I think I know how to make people smile. I could even make you smile, Hollowbeak. Is that enough for you?'

And then Melodie Rose began to hum

again, a song she almost remembered her father singing her.

The sky brightened a little above them both as Melodie hummed.

And Hollowbeak, to his astonishment, realised he knew the song. Someone had sung it to him, long ago. Someone he'd loved very much.

Hollowbeak decided then, finally, that, *yes*, he would help her. This strange, long-boned, too-solid sunshine girl. Though he might not tell her straight away. She might bother him more, for assistance and solutions, if he told her straight away.

But he would help her.

It is nice, he thought to himself, with no small amount of shame, *to be needed. I haven't felt that for a while.*

And then he thought, *It might be nice to smile.*

8

The Lady in White

The next day, Melodie crouched below the silver birch tree, her arms folded about herself, and she stared through the leaves at Hollowbeak the crow.

She would sit here, she would stare, until he agreed to help her.

She knew he would help her.

Melodie knew more things about crows than what she had told Hollowbeak. She knew that they could use tools and that they were brave enough to chase off eagles. She knew that they sometimes caused power blackouts and they could also hold grudges.

She also knew that a crow could not *resist* a project. And Melodie Rose had given Hollowbeak the most important project of all – saving his home.

Of course, he would help her. It was only a matter of *when*.

Staring would help. She could see she was already starting to turn him. His feathers were all ruffled and sometimes he went, *Harrumph*.

He would turn, sure as eggs, and this gave her *hope* – some small amount of hope that they could win against this mysterious Lady in White.

Melodie needed the hope. She needed to win this. She *needed* to save Direleafe Hall.

She needed to save it because she had arrived on its doorstep with a note pinned to her coat and a broken heart and no memory, and, after only a few days here, she felt her heart mending.

Her grandmother mended it, with her cups of tea.

Her warm cosy bed mended it.

And the ghost girls mended it, too. They were her friends. They were like her. And they liked her. (Well, Lucy and Florence did. She wasn't too sure about Nell.)

And there was the other thing, of course. The thing Nell had told her. It wasn't only that if you died in a place, you were stuck there. It was also that, if the place where you were stuck no longer existed, then, well, neither did *you*.

Nell and Lucy and Florence seemed to think that she was their saviour, but she wasn't sure she was at all. How could a humming, fact-filled thing with little memory to speak of be a saviour of *anything*, let alone a whole school?

Melodie couldn't do it alone. But she suspected she wouldn't have to.

Hollowbeak flew down to sit beside Melodie. *She's coming*, was all he said.

Melodie raised an eyebrow at him, and he sighed in a put-upon way. *All right*, he said, *I'll help you.*

'Most excellent crow,' whispered Melodie.

She watched around the tree trunk. At first, there was only a blur in the distance – kitten-white and indistinct. But soon the blur took the form of a woman, tall and thin and formidable.

As she walked towards Melodie, through the high gates and up the rocky, weed-choked path, Melodie saw who she truly was.

The white was a suit, and she wore it like paladin armour. Her pale hair was lacquered to her skull like a helmet. Her face betrayed no emotion. Her cheekbones were arrowheads, her eyes like steel and midwinter frost.

Melodie wondered, as the lady *clip-clopped* past, if that hair would protect the lady's head at all if *someone* were to throw something *awfully hard* at it.

Not Melodie, of course. Melodie wasn't violent. She knew this about herself. But Aeschylus, in Ancient Greece, had died when an eagle dropped a tortoise on his head. She looked at the sky. There were eagles up there sometimes. It was *possible.*

In clumps, all along the grass, the other Direleafe girls stared at the lady, fascinated. They whispered to each other, excitedly. They didn't know who the lady was, so they made up stories.

'She's a billionaire philanthropist. She's going to buy us a lap pool!'

'She's an international woman of mystery! She's spying on us, for the bad guys!'

'She's an Indian aristocrat. She's giving us a tiger!'

None of them were right, of course. Melodie and her ghost friends were the only ones who knew who the Lady in White really was ...

The person who would flatten Direleafe Hall.

Ms Gallow welcomed the lady with a wary smile and invited her into the hall ...

When Ms Gallow showed her back out again, her smile had disappeared. The twinkle in her eye was nowhere to be seen. It looked as though sadness had overtaken her whole entire soul.

Go to her, said Hollowbeak.

Melodie emerged from behind the tree. She walked up the stairs to Ms Gallow. 'What's wrong, Grandma?' she said. And even though she knew the answer, she asked, 'Who was that woman?'

'That woman,' her grandmother said, sadly, 'has bought Direleafe Hall.'

'*Has* bought?' Melodie asked. Florence had only said *trying to buy*.

Ms Gallow nodded. 'It's finalised, now. The deal is done.'

Melodie gasped. 'But where will I go?'

Ms Gallow shook her head. 'I know you've only just arrived here, Melodie Rose. But you needn't fret. You will go wherever I go. And where we go next ...' She laughed, joylessly. 'At least it might have working electrics.'

'But ... I *can't* go,' Melodie blurted. And then, when her grandmother looked at her curiously, she added, 'The note. It said I belong here. And I *like* it here. And what about the girls?'

Her grandmother sighed. 'Come with me inside, won't you? I think I need some tea.'

Inside Ms Gallow's office, the room was lit by the gentle glow of candles. Ms Gallow sat on her desk chair, a leather diary before her and a filing cabinet behind. Melodie perched on a rotating chair and resisted the urge to spin.

Now was not a time for spinning.

'I have always taught at Direleafe Hall,' Ms Gallow told Melodie. 'I can't imagine myself without this place.'

Melodie cradled her mug. It warmed her fingertips. 'Why does it have to be like this?' she asked her grandmother. 'It's not *right*.'

'Because,' said Ms Gallow, 'I am old, and this place is old, and nobody wants a place like this anymore. And nobody wants a teacher like me. They want new schools and new teachers who know about all the new ways of doing things.

They want things that are shiny and only last until the next shiny thing comes along.'

'She's very shiny,' Melodie said. 'The lady who is buying this place. All shiny and white and clean. But Nell said ... I mean, I *heard* that she has been here before, many times, and that you turned her away. Why, *this* time, did you say yes?'

Ms Gallow inclined her head. 'Perhaps now I have something else,' she said, 'to look after, aside from this hall.' She looked intently at Melodie.

'But ...' Melodie scrabbled for answers, for excuses and reasons. 'But I might not even stay with you for awfully long,' she settled on, finally. 'My mother ... my mother might return.'

'Oh, darling,' said Ms Gallow.

'I belong here,' Melodie said, feebly. 'This is my home. Your home. Our family's home.'

And Melodie understood by the look in her grandmother's eyes that Ms Gallow knew something more than Melodie did, about her mother.

Her grandmother shook her head. 'Direleafe Hall has escaped the flattening much longer than it should have. But now is our time. And we will be a memory. And then we won't even be that.'

'I can fix it,' Melodie whispered.

Ms Gallow sighed. 'You are a dear creature,' she said. 'But it's better this way.'

'Please don't give up,' Melodie said.

Her grandmother looked away, across to the fields or maybe to some memory, visible only to her, and she said, finally, 'A woodpecker can break down even the most ancient tree if it has enough time.' She looked back at Melodie. 'And I am a very old tree, Melodie Rose.'

'There's an old ash tree I read about,' Melodie said, quietly. 'Its name is Still Sorrow. It is so tall it towers above the other trees. As though it's watching over them all, protecting them.’ She met her grandmother’s eye. ‘I bet a woodpecker couldn’t fell Still Sorrow,’ she said. ‘Never in a million years.’

9
Conkers

'How did you help Wonder Quinn?' Melodie asked Hollowbeak.

She perched, the next day, with the bird in the silver birch tree. The other ghost girls sat nearby, at the gates of Direleafe. Nell was telling Lucy off for daydreaming while she spoke. Lucy mumbled apologies, and Florence ignored the both of them. She was crouched down, examining beetles.

Hollowbeak watched them, curiously. *There is something familiar about those girls*, he thought, *but I can't put a feather on it.* His memory, from long ago, was hazy now. That can happen when a heart breaks.

What did you say? he asked Melodie when she poked at his downy breast.

'Wonder Quinn,' Melodie said. 'Perhaps the clues for saving Direleafe Hall lie in how you helped her.'

What do you know about Wonder? Hollowbeak asked.

Melodie shrugged. 'She was the ghost girl who you set free.'

I didn't set her free, he said, with a voice as sticky as tar.

I never wanted her to be free, he thought. *I wanted her to stay with me.*

Instead, he huffed, *Wonder Quinn helped her own self. And, well ...* He tilted his head. *A girl called Mabel Clattersham helped her some, also. And, if you must know, she did it with a list.*

That's it! thought Melodie Rose. *Lists!*

And, suddenly, a memory crackled into view within her.

★

Her father, sitting at a kitchen table, a notepad and pen before him.

'What are you doing?' Melodie asked. She looked over his shoulder.

Doctor Aboud
Five times a day
If any pain, call immediately

Her father covered the page with his hand. 'I'm making lists,' he told her. 'Of all the kinds of bears that exist in the world today.'

'But there's something about a doctor ...'

'Oh, that's just the old scrap I'm writing on,' her father said, waving a hand. 'Stuff from years ago. Bears is what I'm doing today.'

'So, tell me,' said Melodie, grinning. 'Tell me all the kinds of bears.'

Her father pulled her close to him. 'Only if you sing me a song,' he said. 'A song of your heart. Your songs make the stars glow brighter and my heart grow as big as the world. Sing me a song, my darling girl – the ballad of Melodie Rose.'

★

The memory faded – a fingerprint blurring it.

Melodie blinked. Hollowbeak was peering at her. *What is it?* he asked.

She shook herself. 'Nothing,' she whispered. 'I was just thinking of lists.'

Above them – though they could not see it because the sky was blue – a star burst into being.

Lists, said Hollowbeak.

Melodie nodded. '*Lists,*' she echoed back.

She smiled. Lists weren't a solution in and of themselves, but they were paving stones on the way to one.

'Benjamin Franklin liked lists,' she said. She hummed for a while, thinking, and then she went on. 'We shall write a list for how to defeat the Lady in White and save Direleafe Hall. And the ghost girls and I won't cease to exist, and my grandmother ...'

Will smile again? Hollowbeak suggested, remembering. *Saving the school will make Ms Gallow happy again.*

'No,' replied Melodie, shaking her head.

'There's a sadness in her, buried deep inside, like swallowed ice that's made its way by accident to her heart. I think ...' She scrunched her face. 'I think it's something to do with my mother.'

She stared for a moment, into the air, trying to see her mother's face, trying to remember her smiling.

Melodie? asked Hollowbeak.

Melodie nodded, decisively. 'A list is how we will do this. I know about lists. It's true – Nell said I knew things and I do, only some of the things are smudgy.' She ruffled Hollowbeak's feathers. 'All black and smudgy, just like you.'

Hollowbeak muttered some words below his breath as he straightened his feathers back out.

'Did I make you mad, little black bird?' whispered Melodie. 'I'm sorry. I know how to cheer you up. Did you know that antelopes—' She didn't get to tell Hollowbeak just what it was that antelopes could do, because that was when someone threw a conker at the tree. It hit Melodie on the head.

At first, she thought it might be a tortoise – because of all that thinking she'd been doing about Aeschylus. She was rather disappointed to see it was only a conker. She rubbed at the spot where the nut had glanced her temple and looked down below her for the culprit, for the villain.

Two long black plaits flew through the sky, like willow leaves caught on the wind.

Melodie knew those plaits.

Ines Amontillado!

Melodie watched as the dark-haired imp ran away in the direction of another girl. A bird-boned, pale little wisp of a girl. Melodie remembered her from the first night in the refectory – *Rowan Underhill.*

Melodie watched as Ines Amontillado threw another conker, right at Rowan's head. This conker *connected* and blood made a scarlet rivulet on Rowan's flurry-white skin.

Rowan cried and cried as Ines marched off into the shadows.

'That was very mean,' Melodie gasped. 'Why did she do that?'

Ines Amontillado seems like a very mean girl, Hollowbeak said. *It is most unkind indeed, to throw a conker at a person. At* two *people.*

Melodie shook her head. 'Oh, no. She didn't throw a conker at *me.* How could she when I'm a ghost? Perhaps she was aiming for you.'

You could throw a conker back, said Hollowbeak, mildly. *Or a rock.*

Melodie shook her head. 'I'm not unkind,' she said. 'But she can't be allowed to behave like that! I'll find a solution, though, to Ines Amontillado.' She wiped at her throbbing temple and her fingertips came away red.

And she didn't notice the black bird beside her, giving her a curious look.

10
Lists

Later that night, a compress held against the growing welt on her forehead, Melodie began work on the list, her friends by her side. She held a candle and listened out for her grandmother's footsteps in the hall. Her grandmother had gone to bed long ago, but Melodie knew by now how little she actually slept.

Sometimes, Ms Gallow paced the halls at night-time. 'No books beneath the covers,' her grandmother had said at bedtime, a hint of a smirk at the corner of her mouth.

'Of course not,' said Melodie. 'It's too risky, anyway, with only a candle to see by.'

A cloud passed over her grandmother's face, but she did not explain it.

Nell, Lucy and Florence were supposed to be helping Melodie, but mostly they were preoccupied with squabbling over stars.

'They're plasma,' said Florence, mildly. 'Everybody knows. Giant glowing balls of plasma held together by their own gravity.' She arched an eyebrow. 'And the ones we see are many, many years dead.'

'They can't be *dead*, silly,' Nell said. 'How can a dead thing glow like that? And *plasma* isn't even a word.'

'I always thought they were where we go,' said Lucy, dreamily. 'When we die, I mean. I always thought the stars were our ancestors and friends long gone, and when we die—'

'*Both* of you are silly,' Nell grumbled. 'You both know one half of nothing at all.'

Melodie had given up trying to make them concentrate. It was hard enough to concentrate *herself*, given all this talk of stars. Melodie knew so many facts about stars she had to bite her tongue so they wouldn't spill out of her.

Hollowbeak helped Melodie with the list. Only, he didn't. He dictated to Melodie, and Melodie dutifully transcribed. But then, with frustrated scratching, she erased every one of his ludicrous ideas. This was the list they made:

1. ~~Throw a rock at the Lady in White's head.~~ (I won't throw a rock at her head because that would be cruel and, no, I won't let Hollowbeak drop a tortoise either. An accidental tortoise might be a nice happenstance, but statistically unlikely.)
2. ~~Put rabbit scats in her pockets.~~ (I won't do that either, even if Hollowbeak collects them for me. There's got to be a better way to save Direleafe Hall — a way that doesn't involve rocks or tortoises or dung.)
3. ~~Glue her shoes to the path through the fields so she will be stuck there for always.~~ (Now you're just being silly, Hollowbeak, and, besides,

a person can escape from their shoes if they really set their minds to it. But I suppose I can't expect you to know that, given you are a bird.)

Hollowbeak was kind to try to help, Melodie thought, but suggesting all these minor cruelties did nothing but fill her with prickles.

'I don't like cruelty,' Melodie said as she scratched the last one out. 'Now, are you going to be properly helpful?'

Hollowbeak grumbled because he was Hollowbeak. But he also made sure to sigh and say, *If I must.*

And Melodie began a new list:

1. Show the Lady in White how delightful Direleafe Hall really is.
2. Appeal to her humanity.
3. ~~Poison her.~~

'Definitely not!' cried Melodie. 'Only villains poison.'

'Doll's eye flowers do it, too,' said Florence, airily. 'And belladonna, and columbines, and angel's trumpet – they poison but not *intentionally*, naturally, because they are plants and plants have no sentience, as far as we—'

All right, all right, you clever thing! said Hollowbeak, and there was something in his eye like a joke, then. He turned back to Melodie and whispered, *But what if we* were *to find some columbines—'*

'No!' cried Melodie Rose.

All right, then, how about blackmail?

Melodie narrowed her eyes at him. 'Blackmail is for villains, also.'

There has to be something *terrible about her*, Hollowbeak continued, as if Melodie had never spoken. *We must find out something terrible and use it to coerce her.*

'But, Hollowbeak, that sounds so spiteful,' said Melodie.

She wants to flatten us, snapped Hollowbeak.

Melodie looked at him. 'I thought this was

my project,' she said. 'And you were a reluctant helper.'

Hollowbeak did not say what he was thinking, which was this: *I have always belonged to Direleafe Hall. Ever since I can remember, it's been my home, my comfort, my safety, my memory. I will not let it be flattened.*

Yes, Melodie had begun all of this, had cast on the first row, but he ...

He was tangled in it, now.

He nodded at the paper. *Write it down.*

Melodie sighed. 'All right, then,' she said.

3. ~~Poison her.~~ Find out something terrible about the Lady in White and use it for blackmail.
4. Scare her away.

Number four was Hollowbeak's last suggestion. He looked to Melodie, after he gave it, expecting her to forbid it. But she didn't.

'Last resorts,' she said instead. 'Only for last resorts.'

'How are you going to do any of that?' Florence asked. 'How are you going to do anything about anything, when *you* are a ghost, and *you* are a bird? There's no point having a list if you don't know how to do any of the things on it. It's illogical.'

'I'm worried,' Lucy said, her chin trembling. 'I'm worried that neither of you will work out how to fix this, and Direleafe Hall will be squashed and crumbled. And then we will disappear.'

Melodie tried to quell the insistent voice within her – the one that said Lucy was right.

The one that said, *You can't fix this.*

The one that said, *You couldn't fix him. You couldn't fix him, and he fell.*

The one that showed her a memory.

★

Her mother, running into the street, her face all twisted and howling.

Melodie, lying on the ground, all bruised, all bloodied, but her mother did not see her.

And later, Melodie cried and cried, but her mother did not see her, still.

★

Melodie stared out the window, blinking back tears as the memory smudged itself. As she watched, three new stars appeared in the darkness and these stars shone the brightest.

'That won't happen,' said Melodie, forcing a smile as she turned back to her friends. 'We *will* nut it out.'

'How?' said Lucy, sobbing.

'How?' said Florence, crossing her arms. 'And I want logic, please.'

'How?!' yelled Nell, stomping her foot on the floor. 'I need more than lists and declarations! I need a *how*.'

Melodie Rose felt all tightly wound. Her chest was full of barbed wire and her brain was thistles and thorns, and everything inside her vibrated. She opened her mouth to reply to Nell but, instead, a note emerged, pure and sweet and resounding.

In the night sky, the small clutch of stars seemed to brighten, to come closer to better hear her.

And Melodie clasped her mouth with her hand, her eyes wide and fearful.

'What was *that*?' gasped Nell.

'It sounded like an angel,' said Lucy.

'It did,' Florence whispered, and everyone stared at her, for this was a most unscientific thing to say.

Melodie lowered her hand. 'I don't know,' she whispered. 'I think ... I think I can sing.'

'Try again,' Nell commanded.

And Melodie did. She opened her mouth and concentrated as hard as she could but this time ... all that emerged was a hum, wavering and reedy. 'I don't remember how to do it,' she said.

Nell's eyes narrowed. 'Could you sing before? *Before* you died?'

Melodie shook her head. 'I don't remember ...'

★

Her father, swinging her around in the kitchen and a voice singing a song about summer and her mother laughing, laughing ...

Her mother saying, 'Never stop singing, my sunrise. Ever.'

★

'I need some air,' Melodie gasped. She held out her arm to Hollowbeak. 'Will you come with me?' she asked.

I will, said Hollowbeak. *But I don't need to be carried. I'm not a pet.* The small black bird flew past the wooden sill and off into the night. There were seven stars in the sky now, shining brightly.

And when he had gone, Melodie turned to walk past her friends and found them peering, curiously, at her forehead.

'Do you know,' said Nell, in a voice low and wondering, pointing at the spot where Melodie's compress had been, 'I don't think I've ever had such a wound, in the whole time since my death.'

11
Past midnight

Melodie and Hollowbeak sat on the front steps of Direleafe Hall. It was past midnight. Melodie liked the way the cool air felt on her skin. Like so many tiny, stroking fingers. Like feathers. Like tears.

I always did like how the moonlight turns everything silver, whispered Hollowbeak. *It makes everything glitter. Even Direleafe Hall looks beautiful in the moonlight.*

Melodie was busy breathing. She let the air fill her lungs then leave them, taking some of her worries with it.

It took her a moment to properly hear

what Hollowbeak had just said. When she did, Melodie turned to Hollowbeak, mouth open, the skin on her arms all prickling.

'That's it!' she said. 'We should make the Lady in White stay here at night-time to show her how delightful Direleafe Hall *really* is. Then she won't see the dampness or the mould or the way everything is breaking down. She'll only see the silver of it all, the glowing.'

Living people don't like the moonlight as much as dead ones do, said Hollowbeak, rolling his button eyes. *Living people like golden things, like sunsets and sunrises.*

Melodie closed her eyes, and she saw, inside of her, so big it filled her up entirely, a sunrise – pink as a peach.

And she felt ...

She could *feel* an arm around her, strong and warm and safe.

★

'Did you know that, technically, sunrise lasts only an instant?' Melodie said. 'I read it in a book. The

moment when the sun appears on the horizon – that's sunrise, truly. The rest is just glow.'

She looked up at her father, who smiled down at her.

'Then enjoy it,' he said. 'Enjoy the instant. Life is an instant, Melodie Rose.'

'That's sad,' she replied to him.

He shook his head. 'No. The glow is a memory of a sunrise. An echo. But it's the most beautiful part. Sometimes, memories are the most beautiful part.'

'I'll always remember this,' Melodie said. 'Always and forever.'

'So will I,' her mother said, leaning against the doorway. 'You are my two sunrises.'

★

'I love sunrises, too,' Melodie whispered to Hollowbeak, looking up at the sky. Was there another star there, or did she only imagine it? 'Even more than midnight.'

Hollowbeak inclined his head. *Of course you do,* he said.

'The Lady in White will adore this place at sunrise.'

Hollowbeak shook his head. *Even if that's true, it would never work, Melodie Rose. How will we ever get her to come here at sunrise?* He waved a wing. *It's a distraction and it will never work.*

Melodie peered down at him. 'You said you would help me,' she reminded him. 'I *need* you to help. I need you to bring her here. You're the only one who can roam from this place.'

How could I *possibly do that? How could I bring her here – a whole human – all the way to Direleafe Hall?*

'You've been to the stars,' she reminded him, 'and you think you can't do this?'

I went to the stars and was turned away, he countered.

'You're the only one who can do it,' Melodie repeated. She slithered down the stairs so she was lying flat on the cobblestone path, using the step as a pillow. 'The only one who can leave.

And you can *fly*, Hollowbeak! How astonishing that must be,' she said, 'to have always been able to fly.'

Not always, he said, very quietly. And then his eyes grew faraway and, in that moment, Melodie saw something almost human about him.

Curious, she thought.

But I'm a bird, now, he pointed out, finally. *I am only a bird and I am very small.*

'Birds can fly ... down chimneys,' Melodie said, gleefully. She sat up. 'Birds can fly down chimneys and they can deliver notes. *That's it!* I will write a note that says the lady must come here at sunrise, and you will fly down the Lady in White's chimney and leave the note on her pillow. Then she will read the note and she will come here ...' She spoke grandly, now. 'At sunrise, as commanded, because who, Hollowbeak, *who* could ever refuse a mysterious note that said they had to be at a place at *sunrise*? It's as you said – the living love a sunrise, and they love a mystery, too! Refusing a note like that would be madness.'

Sending a note like that would be madness, Hollowbeak grouched.

Melodie turned so she was facing away from him. She began to hum, softly, sadly, and the song seemed to make something within Hollowbeak soften.

He sighed. *I will do it,* he said. *But I don't know where to go. How will we find out where the Lady in White lives?*

'Easy,' said Melodie, turning back, grinning. 'She must have left a business card or sent a letter or *something* that has her address on it. My grandmother keeps everything that's important. She's fastidious about it.'

How do you know that? asked Hollowbeak.

★

Her mother had made a mess again – crystals and cards and candles all over the floor.

'I thought we would keep the new house tidy,'

her father said, with a smile. 'I thought we agreed on that.'

Her mother laughed. 'I never agreed. Dull women keep tidy houses.' She shook her head. 'No, that's not true. My mother was tidy but never dull.'

'Tell me more about my grandmother,' Melodie said, crawling onto her mother's paint-spattered lap. 'Tell me about how she was tidy.'

'Well, she was *very tidy,' her mother said, smiling, with a distant look in her eyes. 'And organised. And she kept things. Not mess or clutter ...' Her mother waved a hand. 'The important things. Photographs. Letters. All of that. Everything except ...' She laughed. 'For me.'*

'She ... discarded you?' Melodie asked, searching for the most perfect word.

Her mother's face grew serious, and then she shook her head. 'No,' she said. 'She set me free. All the best mothers do.' Her face brightened again. 'Sing me a song, Melodie Rose. Sing me a song while I tidy.'

★

'I just know,' said Melodie. She tapped her chin. 'But *where* would she keep it? Not in the cottage. There are no school things in there.'

And the archives burned down, said Hollowbeak, sadly. *Her office?* he suggested. *But it will be locked. And it's up all the stairs, past the bedrooms of the girls. One of them will wake. One of them will run down to the cottage and alert your grandmother.*

'I will be quiet as a mouse.' Melodie pulled a pin from her blood-red hair. 'And I know how to pick locks.' She tilted her head, remembering a book with a stone-grey cover. She could *see* her fingers turning the pages. She could almost *taste* the pickle sandwich she ate while reading. 'I read the procedure in a book of facts,' she said to Hollowbeak. 'Did you know that in Ancient Rome, women were the keepers of the keys? They wore them as jewellery. Isn't that fascinating?'

Hollowbeak looked away from her, and Melodie followed his gaze up to the sky, where the cluster of stars seemed to be expanding. He didn't say anything for an awfully long time, until he said this: *I did not know that, Melodie Rose. But I did know that* all *the best girls know how to pick locks.*

12
Ms Gallow's office

The pin in the lock jiggled and clicked. The sound, in the dark, quiet hallway, was a thunderclap, a siren.

Melodie waited, still as a fox in a hunter's crosshair.

She didn't need a candle to see by – the family of stars who watched her through the window seemed to burn more brightly as she walked up the hall, as if they wished to help her.

She waited for her grandmother to come, led by Ines or Rowan, sleep-rumpled and bewildered and full of questions. She waited, breathless, for her grandmother's eyes to fill with fury and disappointment, for her to say to Melodie, 'I think it's time.'

And Melodie would say, 'For what?'

And her grandmother would say, 'Just time.'

'Just time ...' Melodie whispered. And her hand, at the lock, froze.

★

The morning light in the kitchen was speckled silver, filtered through a window that was never quite clean.

Melodie sat at the kitchen table, poring over a book so thick it hurt her arms to lift it. This book had facts about birds in it.

Her mother was dancing, which should have been a joyous thing, used to be a joyous thing, but now when her mother danced, it was sad. As she danced, she kept one eye, always, on the man in the photograph – the man with the Fred Astaire eyes – who was gone, who had fallen.

Melodie could still feel it on her skin, like a scar. How he had touched her, and how that touch had gone.

And Melodie had fallen, too, and she had hit her head, and her head still hurt, but that wasn't the part that hurt most.

She tried to chase away the memory of it with facts about eagles and with a song. But when she opened her mouth, she couldn't sing. She hadn't been able to since her father died.

Instead, she hummed.

She hummed, as her mother danced.

Usually, her mother liked her singing, so she thought she might like her humming, too. She thought it might make her smile.

Melodie was good at making people smile.

Today, her mother would not stop crying – she had not stopped since her husband fell.

Usually, her mother asked her to sing more, longer, more loudly.

Today, she just whispered, 'Stop.'

The song on the record player ended with a moan, and her mother stopped dancing.

A cloud passed in front of the sun.

Melodie's mother seemed to be shaking,

seemed as if she might fall.

'I think my heart is gone,' Melodie heard her whisper. 'I think I am gone away with it. I feel like there will be no more sunrises.'

'I can find your heart,' Melodie declared. 'I can find your heart and I can fix you. I'm good at fixing things. I've learned how to fix almost everything, from books ...'

Her mother shook her head. 'You can't fix this,' she said. 'Grief is a thing that can't be fixed.'

'It can!' Melodie pleaded. 'I can do it, Mama – please.'

'No!' her mother insisted, tears falling one by one from her long eyelashes. 'Please stop. Please stop talking, Melodie Rose. Just stop.'

Melodie nodded. Melodie stopped. And she thought to herself, If I'd only stopped talking that day, I might have noticed my father was sick. I could have stopped him from falling.

Her mother said, 'I think it's time.' And then she nodded, and she said, again, 'It's just time. We're going now.'

★

'I wish she would come back,' Melodie said to herself. Then she shook her head. 'She won't. She has nothing to come back for. Because I am a ghost. If I wasn't ... then ...?'

Melodie jiggled the pin again. A beam of starlight seemed to shine right on the lock, and Melodie whispered to it, 'Thank you.'

And Ms Gallow did not come. Because Melodie was as quiet as a mouse, as a ghost. Because the pin did not wake one of the girls, and neither did the turning of the knob or the soft *click* as the door gently closed.

Neither did the opening of drawers. The quiet shuffling of papers.

And neither did the muted sob when Melodie saw the photograph.

She knew immediately who the girl in the photograph was, of course. She had red hair, just like Melodie's. She stood on the green grass of Direleafe Hall, a smile on her face as big as the sky. She seemed so happy, so at home.

Why did she ever leave this place?

Eventually, Melodie found a business card inside her grandmother's diary. She wasn't sure, at first, if it was the right one. It was folded in two, and the crease obscured the name but not the address.

But on the back, in her grandmother's hand, there was a note, scratched angrily into the cardstock: *I will not sell!*

'I wish you hadn't changed your mind,' Melodie sighed. 'But I will fix it.' She looked one more time at the photograph and she whispered, 'I will.'

13
Waiting for Hollowbeak

A few nights later, Melodie sat in her bedroom and waited for Hollowbeak to return.

The three other ghosts lay on the floor, pretend-sleeping. They had moved into Melodie's room in Ms Gallow's cottage. They said it felt more like a real home, as if they were real children, as if they had a mother – or grandmother – watching over them.

Melodie had offered them her bed, but they all said they preferred the floor.

'Sometimes, when I roll over, I can almost feel the hardness of it, pressing on my bones,' murmured Lucy, her dark eyes shining with sorrow and joy. 'Sometimes, I can almost *feel.*'

'It's phantom limb syndrome,' Florence had pointed out. 'Only your whole entire body is phantom.'

'I don't mind,' said Lucy. 'Sometimes the feeling of a thing is enough, even if it isn't real.'

The ghosts never properly slept – only pretended, to feel more alive.

This night – this night of waiting for Hollowbeak – Melodie knew she would not sleep at all. 'Flimsy science?' she said to Florence, as an answer for her own weariness.

'I expect so,' said Florence.

There was no science at all, to this night's insomnia. It was only *heart*. Because Hollowbeak was out there, in the sky, in the dark, alone. She had watched him fly over the wrought-iron gates and over the moors and paddocks that surrounded the hall, and then, finally – when he was no more than a dot or a speck of dust – up and up and up, over the hills and away ...

And he had taken with him, in his small, sharp beak, the letter Melodie had written.

Melodie was uncertain about it. She had tried to write others – she had eight other drafts. But every draft had come out wrong and wonky and not like a letter at all.

Every other one of them came out like a song. The first one was about sunrise and the second one was about stars. There was one about her mother and one about Ms Gallow and even one about Ines Amontillado.

None of them were official enough to appeal to someone like the Lady in White. And why was her heart giving her songs instead of letters anyway? The seventh draft she wrote was still not what was needed. But Melodie had loved the words of this song – they felt right and good and true.

In the morning, we are born, full of stardust,
Still in a dream cocoon.
And the stars are our mothers and fathers

Who shield us against the gloom.
And we sing a sweet song to the sunrise
And we sing our goodbyes to the moon
We touch the window of our warm, safe home
And the stars whisper, 'We'll see you soon.'

But when she opened her mouth to sing them, all that emerged was a hum.

She threw the paper to the floor in disgust and despair.

Then, she picked up her pen again, and she wrote a proper letter. Formal and official, the sort of thing the Lady in White would esteem.

She even used the words *posthaste*, suggested by the clever Florence, and *aforementioned,* suggested by Hollowbeak. She had felt very grown up, writing down those words. They sounded like something a duke might say, when sending off a missive, with one of those old-fashioned postmen who rode horses because there were no bicycles until 1817 (Melodie knew this from books).

For the lady who wants to buy Direleafe Hall,

This here is a *remarkably* magical note, written by magical folk.

We have an important message for you, and you must pay it the *utmost attention.*

Your presence is required at *the hall aforementioned!*

Here, in the *beginning of things* as the sun is born, you will see all the wonders that cannot be observed in the cowed middle age of day.

Here, you will see a shining, glowing, *golden* place, where dreams of the coming hours are sparked into life, and happiness, too, and it is *imperative* that you come — straight away! — on receipt of this note. You must be here, at dawntime, exactly, to observe all the wonders.

And when you observe them, you will see:

Direleafe Hall is a place worth loving. A place worth saving.

Come! Posthaste! We so eagerly await your arrival!

Signed and sincerely,

The Magical Folk of Direleafe Hall

Hollowbeak said the letter was *adequate*, and Melodie took this as a compliment.

You must try to get some sleep, until I get back, he told her. *The feeling of no sleep – of staying up all night – is terribly hard to bear. For humans at least, for children.* He cleared his throat. *It feels like one's skin is filled with sand.*

'How do you know that?' Melodie asked. 'About the sand? It's not as if *you* were ever a human child.'

Hollowbeak did not reply. Perhaps he did not hear her.

Melodie had tried to do as he'd asked her. But even though her bed was as comfortable as clouds, all she really wanted to do was think of other songs to sing and look up at the stars.

She thought she could count twenty-seven, now.

And then dawn came, and Hollowbeak had still not returned.

14
The second one, I suppose

Melodie counted the minutes, and Hollowbeak did not appear. She counted thirty of them in total.

And though the landscape was dark outside, it was lit up in places by the daybreak. So, Melodie might not have seen him on the hill, but she would have seen him by that apple tree. Or above that small, huddled cluster of sheep. Or just a glimpse of him as he flew over the wrought-iron gates – it was quite bright over there.

But ...

He did not come.

He did not come.

He did not come.

And Melodie's eyes grew droopy. And the film projector in her mind clicked into life.

★

She sat at the kitchen table, waiting for her mother and father.

She sat there and she waited until the sky grew dark.

Finally, she lay her head down on her palms and fell asleep.

When she woke, her mother sat before her, staring at her father's photograph. 'He has Fred Astaire eyes,' she whispered.

'Where is he?' Melodie asked. 'Where is Papa? I have a song to sing him.'

Her mother did not reply.

And her father did not come.

He did not come.

He did not come.

★

Melodie blinked and squinted.

The sky was brighter now – another new star had appeared – but still there was no Hollowbeak.

But then ...

Wait!

There, in that yawning patch of morning light, just over the rise. The smallest speck. And then a dot.

And then a bird, soaring – unmistakeably a bird – and it was a black bird, and it *was* Hollowbeak, and he was at the gate, now ...

At the wall ...

At the window, and ...

Why did he look so sad?

'What?' she said to him as she pushed up the pane.

He shook his head. *I'm sorry,* he said. *She wasn't there at the address Ms Gallow had in her desk.*

'Wasn't there? Was ... on holiday, perhaps?'

Hollowbeak shook his head. *The place was empty, as if nobody had ever been there at all.*

Melodie nodded. She swallowed and, putting Hollowbeak on her arm (he let her, this time), she closed the window and went back to her bed.

Hollowbeak let her stroke his feathers until her breathing slowed.

And then, in the final moment before Melodie slipped away into the shortest of slumbers, she whispered, 'On to the second one on the list, then, I suppose.'

15
Humanity

'It was never going to work,' said Nell. 'It was a terrible plan. I'm beginning to think I was wrong about you, Melodie Rose. Perhaps you're not special at all.'

'I really thought it would work,' said Melodie, sadly. 'I thought the sunrise would make her see how beautiful this place is. I thought the sunrise would make it glow.'

'Direleafe Hall is beautiful *always*,' said Lucy. 'Not only at sunrise.'

'Has she seen the library?' asked Florence. 'Has she seen the antique books?'

'Has she seen the gardens?' Lucy asked.

'Has she seen them in the early morning when the dew turns the whole garden to a place like dreaming? Has she seen the cracks in the cobblestones that look like arteries, like rivers? Has she—'

'Quiet, Lucy!' snapped Nell, and Lucy quietened, swallowing her words like cod liver oil.

But then Nell added, 'Has she seen the desk in Ms Gallow's classroom that has a badger in the grain? It's little things like that – like badgers in desks – that make this place so special.'

Melodie noticed that Hollowbeak flinched when Nell talked about the badger. And then he flew away.

'Little things and little moments,' said Lucy, her eyes shining. 'Tiny moments of joy. Has she seen the tiny moments of joy?'

'I think she has seen everything,' said Melodie, watching as Hollowbeak glided to the silver birch tree, landed on a branch and hid his head beneath his wing. 'She doesn't see it like we do.'

Melodie gestured at the grounds, at the girls jumping in mud puddles, up to their knees, and shrieking with the unbridled joy of it, at girls who were having a picnic on a ragged blanket and at girls playing hopscotch. Rowan was reading a book about elves. Ines was bouncing a ball against the wall, *harder, harder, harder.* And a circle of smaller girls danced and giggled and fell on their backs, exultant.

There weren't many girls, here at Direleafe Hall – not enough for a proper school – but the ones who *were* here were joyful. And besides, Direleafe Hall was not a proper school at all.

It was a home.

'She doesn't see how this school makes us happy,' Melodie whispered. More loudly, she added, 'The dust and the cracks and the dirt and the potatoes are not a sadness. The girls are happy here, despite and *because* of the dirt.

Because dirt makes children happy and so do potatoes. But grown-ups don't see that!'

'*We* don't eat potatoes,' argued Nell, picking at the earth with a stick that made no indents, no furrows, made no mark at all.

'We don't have dirt on our knees,' said Florence, pointing at her translucent kneecap. 'We have no dirt anywhere.'

Melodie looked at her own knees. They were black. She covered them up with her skirt.

'Anyway,' she snapped. 'The point is, she didn't come, so it didn't work, and so it is on to the second one on the list.'

'*Appealing to her humanity*,' said Nell, reading Melodie's list over her shoulder. 'What does that even mean?'

'My father used to say it,' Melodie blurted, and then, just as quickly, she fell silent.

★

'If anyone is ever unkind, appeal to their humanity. Appeal to the small spark within them

that is still made of stardust. That's the purest thing. We are stardust. That's what being human means. If a person is unkind, it's only that they've forgotten. To remind them, show them kindness yourself. Show them joy. If that doesn't work, show them the stars.'

★

Melodie looked up at the clear blue sky, blinking back tears. She could see the ghost of the moon there and, beside it, the ghost of another star.

'We show her how important Direleafe Hall is to all of us,' Melodie said. 'We show her how it gives us joy.'

'The other girls don't see us,' said Lucy. Her chin wobbled a little bit. 'You are the only one who ever saw us. Not even Wonder saw us because she didn't know she was one of us.'

'Flimsy science,' muttered Florence.

Melodie looked away from the ghost girls, and she didn't say the thing that she had been avoiding. She hadn't said it a moment ago. She wouldn't say it now.

She didn't tell Lucy that, sometimes, she imagined that the other girls – the human girls – *did* see her, that Ines really sneered at her, that Rowan really stared, longingly. It was impossible, of course, but all imagining is a beautiful sort of impossible.

And yet ...

Hollowbeak had told her about Mabel Clattersham and how she saw Wonder, even though Mabel was alive and Wonder was dead, and Melodie wondered if it was all tied, tangled and knotted together – a string of ghosts and the girls who saw them, stretched out through forever.

Melodie didn't tell the ghost girls about her imaginings. Something told her that her friends would look at her differently if they knew about that.

But there was the conker ...

That was an accident, though. Ines didn't mean to throw it at her. Melodie was *sure* it was meant for Hollowbeak.

Anyway, it was that – the conker – that had given Melodie the idea.

Melodie Rose knew precious little about Ines Amontillado, but she did know this: Ines Amontillado had not come from a smiling sort of home.

Nell had told her, of course. Nell knew everything about the girls who lived at Direleafe.

Ines Amontillado's father was an army sergeant, Nell told her, and he never, ever came to visit, and he never took Ines home with him.

Melodie felt her heart break for Ines Amontillado when Nell told her that.

But Melodie had spied Ines's expression, more than once, as Ines looked up at Direleafe Hall (when she thought nobody was watching). The anger melted, and her lips twitched with an expression that was close to a smile.

And Melodie knew it, then – despite all of Ines's bluster and bravado and her tendency to be mean – that Ines felt the same way as Melodie did about this funny old place.

Ines Amontillado loved Direleafe Hall. She would not wish this place to be flattened, any more than Melodie would.

'I have a plan,' Melodie told her ghost friends, 'to appeal to the Lady in White's humanity. And I *know* it will work, this time.'

16
A letter to Ines

Dear Ines,

I saw what you did with the conker.

I saw you throw it at Rowan. I saw it hit her head.

I know that if I were to tell Ms Gallow it was you who did it, she would believe me.

She knows you pull hair and whisper curses, Ines. She knows you make other girls cry.

She would believe me.

I will not tell her. I promise. That's not the sort of girl I am.

So, if you think this letter is about blackmail, you're wrong.

This is a letter, actually, with a tantalising

proposition — an *offer* to you, and I think that you might like it.

It is an invitation to an adventure.

Would you like to come on one with me?

But it's more than a simple invitation to adventure, Ines Amontillado. It's an invitation to *help*.

And I think ...

I might be wrong, but I *think* ...

I think you might like to help me.

You see, Direleafe Hall is in trouble, and Direleafe Hall is as important to you as it is to me. It's the only place you have ever belonged — the only place you have ever felt at home.

This place is my home, just as it is yours.

We *both* belong here.

And you can help me to save it!

What do you think, Ines Amontillado?

Would you like to help me save Direleafe Hall?

Melodie placed the note on Ines's pillow, and then, while Ines slept, she whispered to her a song.

It was the song she had begun when she first tried to write a letter to the Lady in White. It had come to her again when she wrote her letter to Ines.

She still could not sing it. But she could whisper. And she could make it *more.*

In the morning, we are born, full of stardust,
Still in a dream cocoon.
And the stars are our mothers and fathers
Who shield us against the gloom.
And we sing a sweet song to the sunrise
And we sing our goodbyes to the moon
We touch the window of our warm, safe home
And the stars whisper, 'We'll see you soon.'
At the dawning, the stars sing a song to us,
And they sing, 'We will watch over you.
We are part of you, you are part of us
And we'll watch as you grow and bloom
And when you sing us your sweet ballad,
We'll sing our song back down to you.'

Ines slept through all of Melodie's song. But when she awoke, she was humming.

17
Ines Amontillado

Ines Amontillado stood at the gates of Direleafe Hall. In front of her, the moors stretched out, on and on and on, until they suddenly disappeared into the sleeping giant hills that surrounded Direleafe Hall.

Ines loved looking at those hills. They felt to her like a barrier, separating her from the man who made her feel small.

Her favourite place in the world, the only place she really loved – though she would never tell a soul – was Direleafe Hall.

She didn't know why she behaved the way she did to the other girls. She just got so angry, sometimes. They were all so bright and happy and smart, and she was so grey inside. She wanted them to see her, and the only way she could was by hurting them.

She didn't want to.

She was only trying to make the hurt inside of herself *less*. She wanted them to like her, but they would not if she was like this.

Ines knew something horrible was happening at Direleafe Hall. She had seen the Lady in White and, once, she saw Ms Gallow crying after the lady left. She had wanted, so badly, to go up to the old woman and hold out her arms and pull her close, but she didn't quite know *how* to do that.

Ines had never been hugged before. Or, at least, not so she could remember. She didn't know how the mechanics of it would work.

Which piece of me goes where?

And she was worried that the old woman would push her away, the way her father had done, the one time she tried it. After all, she was a bad child. A naughty child. And the old woman must hate her.

So, Ines didn't approach Ms Gallow. She only watched from the shadows and wished she could help, somehow.

And then the letter had arrived, on her pillow, and with it the memory of a song.

It took Ines a long time to read it, and some of the words made no sense to her. But she understood the important parts.

The letter made her heart rise into her throat.

Because someone *saw.*

But they said they would not tell.

It made her heart expand.

Because the someone said that Ines could help.

Ines could help save Direleafe Hall.

Her hand shook as she wrote her reply:

OK. I wil do it. wot do I ned to do.

She left the note on her pillow and she fell asleep. And when she awoke, the note was gone, just as she somehow knew it would be, and a flame-red hair took its place.

Now Ines stood at the gates of Direleafe Hall, and she waited with hope in her heart for the Lady in White to arrive.

For her chance to help fix everything.

18
Ines tries

Melodie and Hollowbeak sat in the silver birch tree and looked down on Ines Amontillado.

She was dressed in her Direleafe uniform, with a bright white ribbon in her long dark plait. This had been Melodie's idea, and she had found the perfect ribbon in her grandmother's mending box.

At the end of lunchtime, the day before, Melodie had tied it to the handle of Ines's locker door and crossed her fingers, hoping that Ines knew what to do with it. Melodie was worried she mightn't. She saw how Ines struggled at so very many things. She could not spell very well, or talk without yelling, and she seemed unable to traverse a day without making Rowan cry.

But it seemed that Ines knew exactly what to do with a perfect white ribbon. And she knew how to scrub her face 'til it shone and knew how to smile like an angel, in the face of the Lady in White.

Melodie was quietly impressed.

Melodie and Hollowbeak watched Ines as she smiled, as if she were a virtuous child. They watched as she curtsied. Hollowbeak murmured, *Did you ask her to do that?*

Melodie shook her head as they continued to spy on the scene.

Melodie was good at spying, just as she was good at picking locks. She learned about spying in books. Her father gave her the books. He gave her all the books.

★

The book about spies had a silhouette on its cover – a woman, with a broad-brimmed hat. And when he gave it to her, he said the thing he always said when he gave her a book: 'This will help grow your mind, Melodie Rose. But little moments of joy will grow your heart.'

'Like sunrises?'

He nodded. 'And starlight.'

★

Spying was how Melodie knew when the Lady in White would arrive – an ear to her grandmother's door, an overheard telephone conversation.

You're very clever, said Hollowbeak, grudgingly.

'Thank you,' said Melodie Rose.

They watched, now, beneath a daytime sky that secretly held one more star, as Ines clasped the hands of the Lady in White. They watched as she blinked her pretty eyes – so pretty, Melodie noticed, now that they were not scrunched up in fury. They watched as she told the Lady in White how Direleafe Hall brought her joy. They watched as Ines's pretty, dark eyes made such pretty tears.

They watched and they waited, and they hoped.

But the Lady in White did not take Ines into her arms.

She did not pat her hair or stroke her plaits.

She did not declare to the sky above, 'I have seen the folly of my ways!'

And she made no promises – no proclamations – about the fate of the hall and how it would not be crushed.

And all their hopes became crumbs and ashes.

Instead, the Lady in White grimaced at Ines as if Ines were nothing more than a stinking mess left by an untrained puppy. She gingerly prised Ines's hands from her own, and then, holding her nose in the air, she stalked into Direleafe Hall.

Ines gaped at the woman marching away, and then she let out a growl, as loud as a tiger. She ripped out the ribbon and threw it to the wind. And the wind captured it and lifted it

gently, up and up and up, into the silver birch tree where the ribbon wrapped itself around a spindly branch, until it became a tangled thing that looked more like animal innards.

And when Melodie had finished watching the ribbon, she looked down again at Ines.

And Ines was glowering straight back up at her.

19 Blackmail

Number three? said Hollowbeak later, as the day was ending. The Lady in White was long gone, and the stars were coming out. They came one by one, and it felt, to Melodie, as if they were greeting her. As if they were friends, too. There were three more stars than last time she had counted. Now, they formed a tribe, a village.

Hollowbeak cleared his throat, and Melodie turned away from the stars.

His face was hard, now. He was not the same bird who had joked about poison. He was the sort who might really consider it.

Odious woman.

'Remind me what number three is,' sighed Melodie.

Blackmail, he said. *Blackmail is number three.*

'That's bad,' said Melodie. 'Villainous.'

Not, said Hollowbeak, darkly, *as bad as poison.*

'I don't want to be a bad person,' said Melodie, quietly. 'I want to keep my humanity.'

Hollowbeak stared at Melodie, and he felt something almost like tenderness. *You could never be a bad person,* he thought.

I think, he said, gruffly, *that in this case, Ms Gallow would examine both evils and find the blackmail one lesser. I think, if – when – you save her home, Ms Gallow would think even poison worth it.*

There was a long pause, and then Melodie said, 'We're still not using poison, Hollowbeak.'

Just then there was a crash, like a storm-wave on a rocky beach. Melodie looked out the window to see Ines Amontillado standing in front of a shattered windowpane.

Her heart in her throat, Melodie watched as Ms Gallow approached Ines across the dew-wet grass. Was this the moment when Ines would be banished from Direleafe Hall? Was it all Melodie's fault for getting Ines involved?

But then, Melodie watched as Ms Gallow took Ines into her arms. At first, it seemed as though Ines did not know what to do. But then ... it was as though she *melted* into Ms Gallow.

They stayed there for a very long while.

'I'll do anything,' Melodie whispered, watching. 'I'll do anything to help Ms Gallow. I'll do anything to save Direleafe Hall.'

In the refectory, at dinnertime, Melodie watched the other living girls. She had learned their names, now – there were not many to learn.

She watched as Rebecca smiled shyly at Jean, and Jean smiled shyly back, and Melodie knew that each of them had given their heart to the other.

She watched as Mariam sketched a eucalypt so real that Melodie was sure she saw it sway in an imaginary wind.

She watched as Min made up a silly dance and taught it to Emmanuelle.

She watched as Rowan read a thick leather-bound novel, giggling at times behind her delicate hand.

She watched as the girls laughed and learned and played and fell in love and out and discovered themselves, and she felt, at once, a boundless joy and a sorrow so sharp she clasped her chest.

'I'll do anything,' she repeated to herself. '*Anything* to save this place.'

20 Waiting for Ms Gallow

Melodie Rose had been awake for many hours. She stirred when the sky was still black – morning in night-time's clothing, playing pretend.

'Where are you going?' whispered Lucy.

'I just want to count the stars,' she said.

She climbed out of her window, leaped to the maple tree beside the cottage and shimmied down, down, down. She ran across the moonbeam-shining grass and sat on a stump, halfway between the cottage and Direleafe Hall.

Her grandmother had told her that the stump was once a cherry tree.

Nell had told her that the cherry tree had been cut down after a girl fell from its branches and died.

Florence had whispered, when Nell was out of earshot, that the girl who had died was Nell.

Lucy had sighed, sobbed a little, and told Melodie that she was the one who had asked Nell for the cherries. This was why she was sad – and this was why Nell disliked her so.

'She dislikes me, too,' Florence said. 'But that is because I'm cleverer than she is.'

'She dislikes you,' Lucy said with uncharacteristic braveness, 'because you *told* her not to climb the tree.'

Florence shrugged. 'That's what I said – *I'm cleverer than she is.*'

'I should have been brave and climbed the tree myself,' Lucy sighed. 'I'm never the one who is brave.'

'If you had been, you would have died,' Florence pointed out.

'I died anyway,' said Lucy.

‘Scarlet fever,’ said Florence, lifting her chin. ‘A much more dignified way to die than cherries.’

Maybe it was true, this story, or maybe Lucy and Florence remembered things askew (memory was a funny thing). Whatever the case, the tree was now gone and the stump was Melodie’s sitting place when she woke up before sunrise.

She could have knocked on her grandmother’s bedroom door before the sun had bloomed. She would have been awake. She was always awake, long before sunrise. Perhaps, like Nell and Florence and Lucy, she never properly slept.

Melodie knew it was because of the pupils. Because what if one of them was in trouble? What if one of them got hurt?

What if one ran away, into the moonlight, and never returned to Direleafe Hall?

Melodie looked up at the stars. And she remembered a story her father had told her.

★

'Why do we never go to see my grandmother?' Melodie asked her father. She held out a picture of a building, like a castle, with a laughing-eyed woman standing before it.

'Your mother needed to see the world,' her father told her, sadly. 'She needed to be free and to run.'

'Run? Run from her mother?'

Her father nodded.

'From her home?'

He nodded again.

'Do you think she would ever run from ... us?' Melodie asked.

Her father paused for a very long time. 'She loves you, Melodie Rose,' he said. 'She'll never run from you.'

'But she ran away from this place,' Melodie insisted, pointing at the fairytale building.

Her father nodded again. 'She ran away in the moonlight, with no shoes on her feet. She wanted to see the world. She wanted to find her sunrise.'

'I wish I was her sunrise,' Melodie Rose said, sadly.

Her father kissed the top of her head. 'You are,' he said. 'And you're mine.'

★

Melodie looked up at the sky, blinking quickly.

As if by magic, as she watched, more stars appeared: two, then three, then four. Melodie knew this was strange – stars bursting into being at morning time. But the beauty of it seemed greater than the strangeness.

And they made Direleafe Hall shine even brighter, but it was bright enough without the stars.

Melodie could feel her grandmother, inside the cottage. She could picture her, exactly. She would be standing at her bedroom window, holding a chipped mug of tea. She would gaze through the glass, almost unblinking, as the false night became true morning.

Melodie joined in the communion of watching – as black became indigo, then russet, then apricot and, finally, silver became blue. She hummed to herself the song she'd made up. She wished that she could sing it.

And then, the first lark began its own song, and Melodie thought about larks for a time – about how they symbolise passage from the Earth up to the heavens. When the lark had finished its work for the day, Melodie thanked it and rose from her sitting spot. She rose from the stump that was once the tree that killed the living Nell.

Then Melodie felt a sort of prickling, a tingling on her neck. And she looked back across the grass, towards Direleafe Hall. She saw a shape, in the doorway. She saw a shape that looked like Ines Amontillado.

And then the shape raised a hand.

And Melodie's hand made to wave back.

But that was an impossibility because she couldn't wave *back*, could she? Because Ines was not waving at her.

Because Melodie was a ghost.

Melodie looked behind her but there was no-one else there. She would have said her heart was racing if she had a heart to race.

She turned, quick as a falcon, and ran towards the cottage.

She ran inside the cottage and upstairs, two at a time, and she knocked on her grandmother's bedroom door.

Her grandmother opened the door in the short time it took for Melodie to breathe in and then out. She had one arm in her cardigan and her feet half in her shoes.

'Good morning, dear one,' said Ms Gallow.

Melodie smiled at the thought of being dear.

Ms Gallow said, 'I was on my way to the library. Would you like to join me?'

Melodie nodded because this was exactly what she had hoped would happen.

They walked together, over the grass, and they walked together, into the library. And this is where they were, now, sitting side by side, secretly warm in each other's company.

And Melodie took a deep breath and began with her questions.

21
Questions

'What do you know about the Lady in White?' Melodie asked her grandmother.

The old woman peered at her, her eyes filled with clouds. 'Who?'

'I mean, the lady who's buying Direleafe Hall,' Melodie said, attempting to kick herself in the ankle under the table. By accident, she kicked her grandmother instead.

'What was that?' Ms Gallow gasped.

Melodie replied, 'Oh, a rat, I expect. It definitely wasn't me.'

The old woman narrowed her eyes at Melodie for an exceptionally long time.

‘A rat?’ she said, finally, and Melodie was glad to see the cider-fizz glimmer in her eyes again. She was worried that when it was gone for good, her grandmother might be, too.

‘Well, all right, then. I don’t mind rats. Exceptionally clever creatures.’

Melodie nodded. ‘Plus, they share food with each other, so perhaps they are kind. And they have extraordinary memories ...’ Melodie cleared her throat. ‘I wonder what they remember,’ she whispered. She shook herself. She was getting distracted. ‘Grandma? The lady? What do you know?’

The old woman put down the book she was holding. ‘Why do you want to know about her, Melodie?’

‘I’m a curious sort of girl,’ said Melodie.

‘That you are,’ said the old woman, laughing. ‘But I’m sorry, I can’t help you very much. I don’t know the lady at all.’ The old woman looked away for a moment, her eyes shining. ‘I mean to say, I don’t know her *now* ...’

'What?' said Melodie. 'What do you mean? Did you know her?'

Ms Gallow sighed. 'I did. Once.'

'Really?' said Melodie, her eyebrows lifting. 'When?' And then it came to her, bright as the dawn. 'Was she a Direleafe girl?'

Ms Gallow didn't say another thing, but her face – the sorrow on it – was enough.

'Why would a Direleafe girl want to flatten this place?' Melodie gasped. 'This place is ... it's *good.*'

The old woman shook her head. 'It wasn't for everyone. Perhaps it wasn't for her.'

'Was it not for ... my mother?' Melodie asked, quietly. She knew she shouldn't ask. She knew it had nothing to do with *anything* that she was in here to discover.

But when she closed her eyes, she saw her mother's tears.

When she closed her eyes, she saw her mother's feet, bare.

When she closed her eyes, she saw that

photograph, and in it she had looked *happy*.

Her grandmother's face slackened a little, sadness appearing to wash over her. Melodie did not know what she expected her grandmother to say. She did *not* expect her to say, 'She loved it here.'

'But ... she ran,' Melodie said, confused. 'In the middle of the night. My father told me.'

'You remember that? Him telling you?'

Melodie nodded. 'I remember some things, now. Not everything.'

Her grandmother smiled, sadly. 'Do you remember how much she loved you?'

'I remember her crying.'

'After he died?'

Melodie nodded.

'She loved you more than all the stars in the sky,' her grandmother said. 'You were her north star, Melodie Rose. You were a whole constellation.'

'She told you?'

Her grandmother nodded. 'She wrote to me.'

'Why did we never come to see you?' Melodie asked.

Her grandmother seemed to curl in on herself, wrapping her cardigan tight around her chest as if it were a blanket to comfort her. 'When you were born, she telephoned me. She said she wanted to bring you here to live. I told her to let you see some of the world first. To learn things. To live with your father for a time ... for as long as he had left.'

'You knew ... he was dying?' Melodie gasped. 'You both did? You *all* did?'

Her grandmother nodded. 'I was expecting you both to come and be here forever when I heard.'

There was a long silence, then.

It was broken by the sound of flapping wings.

Melodie looked up to see Hollowbeak, perching on a desk. He was alone for a moment, and then three ghost girls joined him, emerging from the ether.

'Do you know yet?' asked Nell.

'Have you deduced who she is, *really*?' asked Florence.

'We need to know her,' said Lucy, shining-eyed. 'We need to know her ...'

To beat her, finished Hollowbeak. He bobbed over, closer to Melodie. *Ask her name,* he hissed. *If Ms Gallow knows her, I might know her, too. Ask her name.*

Melodie gave them all a befuddled look. She had forgotten entirely, while she talked with her grandmother, the proper reason she was here. It took her mind a moment to make sense of it all.

Hollowbeak rolled his eyes. *Her name,* he repeated.

Melodie cleared her throat. 'What's her name?' she asked. 'The lady? The one buying Direleafe Hall?'

Ms Gallow shook her head. 'It's not important.'

Her initials? Hollowbeak pressed.

Ms Gallow held up a hand before Melodie could speak. 'You don't need to know her name, Melodie Rose. You don't need to concern yourself with any of this.'

'But it *is* my concern! This place is my home, now. And it's my mother's home – you just said so. When she comes back, she'll come back here. We *belong* here. You and me and my mother.'

'Your home is with me,' Ms Gallow corrected. 'Wherever I go, I will take you with me. And your mother will find us when she's ready.'

Melodie shook her head. 'The note said I *belong to Direleafe Hall*.'

Ms Gallow sighed, and her eyes were sparkling again, but this time with sadness. 'Direleafe Hall is only stones. The love within it is made by our souls. Only our souls can make comfort, make safety, make a *home*. Only our hearts can feel love.'

★

Melodie and her mother and father were curled up on a sofa in some other house – some different house. Some other town, some other place her mother had brought them to.

They were smiling, and Melodie ...

Melodie was singing, a song about home.

★

'The lady, when she was a girl ...' Melodie went on. 'She didn't feel love, here. She can't have if she wants to destroy Direleafe.'

'I thought she did,' said Ms Gallow, shaking her head. 'I thought she was happy. She had tiny hearts all over her locker. I thought that meant she loved this place.'

That's it! cried Hollowbeak, with a glint in his eye. *That's who it is. I should have known, and ... I know where she could be.*

And before Melodie could say another word, he had taken flight, up and out of the library window.

'Well,' said Nell. 'Where could that strange bird be off to?'

'He knows who the Lady in White really is,' said Florence. 'He'll be going to her.'

'I think we know who she is, too,' said Lucy, meeting the eyes of her friends. 'We all do.' She shuddered. 'How did we not recognise her?'

'Do you think he will find her?' said Melodie. Then, more softly, she added, 'Maybe this will be the thing. Maybe this will be the *how*.'

Her breath stilled as she noticed the old woman staring. 'Who are you talking to?' Ms Gallow asked.

Melodie shook her head. 'Nobody and nothing,' she said. 'Cobwebs and ... dust.'

Ms Gallow did not look convinced, this time.

Melodie looked out of the window. Hollowbeak was a speck again.

'Why did you ask for her name?' Ms Gallow pressed. 'What does it matter, Melodie Rose?'

'I'm a curious child.'

'So, it's not because you are planning something?' asked Ms Gallow, softly, twinkle-eyed once more. 'Something to save us all?'

Melodie shook her head. 'No,' she replied. 'It's nothing like that at all.'

'I remember,' Ms Gallow went on, looking away and out the window, following Melodie's eyes. 'I remember the day you arrived at Direleafe Hall. I remember thinking it was exactly right, you arriving just at that time. I remember thinking it meant that it was time to finally sell. Time to leave. Perhaps I was wrong about that last part ...' She looked back over at Melodie. 'I was so happy to see you that day.'

'Really?' asked Melodie. 'It didn't look like you thought that. You seemed to look right through me.'

'No,' her grandmother answered, firmly. 'No, I didn't do that.' And then she met Melodie's eye. 'Memory is *such* a funny thing, isn't it? In fact, I think what I said to you, my darling girl, was "Welcome home".'

That evening, at the cottage, Melodie walked to the window. The sky was hung heavy with stars, now – too many to count them all. She shielded her eyes and peered out.

'Who are you looking for?' her grandmother asked.

Melodie tore her eyes away from the dazzling sky – star-full but *empty* – where Hollowbeak was *not*. He'd been gone for such a long time.

'And don't tell me cobwebs. They don't hang on the clouds.'

'I'm looking for a friend,' Melodie whispered.

'Oh, Melodie Rose,' her grandmother said. 'I completely understand.'

Melodie sighed. 'Did you know a crow can travel as much as forty miles in a day?'

Her grandmother shook her head. 'Well, no,' she said. 'I did not know that, Melodie Rose.' Her grandmother joined her at the window. 'Your mother told me you sing,' she said.

'Not anymore,' said Melodie.

'I don't think that's true,' her grandmother

said. 'The song is always inside you. I can see it in there, hiding, wishing to come out again.'

'I've actually ... started writing a song,' Melodie admitted.

'You won't sing it to me?'

Melodie shook her head. 'Maybe soon,' she said.

22 What Hollowbeak saw

Hollowbeak remembered this place. Fifteen Tuberose Lane. It was a small, grey cottage, with a white picket fence. It hadn't changed much, in all these many years.

He had come here, once, long ago, in a fit of spite because he'd wanted to see what sort of place a girl like *that* had come from. Back then, the girl was a bully, the girl was mean, and she was making his favourite girl, Wonder Quinn, sad.

At the time, he thought a girl like that must come from somewhere terrible.

Surely, a girl like that must have come

from unkindness, from a mean, cruel, empty sort of place.

Surely.

Those many years ago, there had been a family here. A husband, a wife, two sons – *her* brothers. There had been a roast dinner on the table, laughter in the air.

Now, there was still laughter in the air, but the woman was old, and the man was older.

On the front porch, the old lady sat with a tabby cat on her knee, humming along to an old-time jazz record. Beside her, there were two children. Only one was alive.

She was happy – the old woman with the cat on her knee. She knew her sons were there, with her (both of them). And inside, her husband's light was dimming, but he still laughed at his 'funnies' on the television.

The old woman had a good, strong pot of tea beside her and three biscuits, which was more than she was meant to have (according to Doctor Daniels), and after her record was finished, she had a good, fat book waiting for her about rakish dukes and duchesses who knew how to fence.

The night was so beautiful. There were so many stars and the world was at peace, for a short time.

The cat was purring and all was well.

But she missed her daughter. She wondered if her daughter missed her.

One day, hopefully, she'd come around, and they could make amends. She hadn't meant it – any of the things she'd said. She hoped her daughter knew that.

It felt as if a piece of her was missing, without her.

Hollowbeak felt it – the *absence* of the daughter – there was no hint or echo of her, anywhere. She was not here, this night. She had not been here for many years.

Where does she live, then?

Not at the address on her business card.

Not at her parents' grey cottage.

Hollowbeak was beginning to think the Lady in White was more of a ghost than any of them.

23 Fixing things

'I can't believe it,' said Melodie Rose. 'I can't believe the Lady in White came from a laughing sort of a home.'

Hollowbeak sat on her shoulder, and they were both secretly happy. Melodie was happy that Hollowbeak had returned, and Hollowbeak was happy that he was on Melodie's shoulder. He would never tell her that, of course.

They were both also discontented and worried about the Lady in White.

'We've got no leads, now,' Melodie said. 'We've got no clues.'

We have a name. I know her name.

'But you're suggesting blackmail,' Melodie said. 'You can't blackmail a person just because you know their name.'

I thought you were against blackmail, said Hollowbeak.

'I am,' said Melodie Rose. She threw up her arms. 'But I'm afraid I'm getting desperate. We have to fight this, Hollowbeak. We have to because nobody else is. Even my grandmother – who loves this place like it was her very own child – is not fighting. We must do it. We just need to find out *how.*'

Perhaps Ms Gallow doesn't know she can fight. Perhaps she doesn't know she's capable.

Melodie stomped a foot, causing the black bird to startle. 'Well, she needs to believe in herself a bit more, doesn't she?' said Melodie. 'She is brilliant and brave, and we all love her, and she fights for us girls every single day. Why doesn't she believe in herself?'

I don't know, said Hollowbeak. *Perhaps it's*

hard to believe in yourself entirely, when a piece of you is missing.

'You mean my mother?' Melodie said. 'So many mothers missing daughters and daughters missing mothers,' she sighed. She looked down at Hollowbeak, her eyes welling. 'And daughters without mothers. Me and Ines and Rowan, too, I suppose, and all those other girls. Where are their mothers and their fathers? If it weren't for this place, where would they be? Where would any of us be? This place *sees* us, and this place *hears* us, and being seen and being heard is what love is, really. It's only when you're seen and heard that you can make a difference and a change and ...'

Melodie broke off, mid-ramble. She could see that Hollowbeak had already stopped listening. He was a million miles away, and perhaps many years ago.

'Hollowbeak!' Melodie called out, startling the bird to attention.

What? What? he squawked.

'Tell me everything you know about her,' she said. 'You know her name and you know where she used to live. Tell me *everything* else.'

For blackmail? Hollowbeak asked.

'For blackmail,' Melodie exhaled, nodding. After a beat, she added, 'Did you know that blackmail comes from Scottish Gaelic words that mean *protection payment*? That's all we're doing, Hollowbeak. We're protecting Direleafe Hall. So, it's not so bad.'

It's not so bad, Hollowbeak agreed, with a nod. *But the things she did – the lady, as a girl – they were very bad indeed.*

Melodie smiled. 'Tell me all of it,' she said.

When Hollowbeak was done, she stood, sharply. 'I need to find my grandmother,' she told the bird. 'I need her to make another appointment with the Lady in White.'

And as she trotted away across to the cottage, she sang her song to herself without even knowing she was doing it.

And the sky above her head was full of starlight.

An hour later, or maybe it was two (time is stringy, elastic, odd when you are a ghost), Melodie saw a chalk-white blur in the distance.

Melodie was waiting on the steps of Direleafe Hall, fear thrumming inside her ribcage. She didn't know how she could go through with it, this terrible blackmail business.

★

Her mother sat at the kitchen counter, drinking a tea that smelled of spices. 'Appealing to humanity is all well and good, my dear,' she told Melodie. 'But if that fails, it's more than fine to fight a little bit dirty. I've had to fight for quite a lot. I've had to fight a little bit dirty for the life I want to live.'

'Is this it?' Melodie asked her. 'The life you want to live?'

Her mother nodded. 'It is. You, my sunrise – you and your father. A new house, every once in a while, and the songs you sing to me. That's all I need for happiness.'

'You'll never run away?' Melodie asked, because she remembered the story of her mother and her bare feet, running in the moonlight.

Her mother's eyes began to shine. 'I can't promise that,' she told Melodie, 'but I can promise I'll always return to you.'

'When? When will you return?'

'When you've learned how to fight some, too, I suppose.'

★

As the Lady in White marched across the cobblestones towards Direleafe Hall, Melodie Rose went down to meet her.

She was ready to fight.

24 Melodie is seen and heard

Most people didn't see Melodie.

But some people did.

Ms Gallow did.

Melodie didn't know why. Perhaps it was some sort of Direleafe Hall magic. Perhaps it was because Melodie wanted her to see her. Melodie chose Ms Gallow.

Or perhaps her grandmother chose her.

But the main thing was, Melodie *wanted* to be seen by Ms Gallow. She didn't want to be seen by the other girls who were pupils at Direleafe Hall because ...

Because ...

Because you are unlovable. Because your mother left you. Because, before, you sang and you talked and you danced, and you were a loud and laughing thing. And your father died, and your mother cried.

It is better to be a ghost.

Melodie did not want the other girls to see her because ... being seen is perilous. Being seen is hard. Being seen is what love is, and love will break your heart.

Perhaps it was true that a ghost can choose who sees it. Hollowbeak had told Melodie that Wonder was seen by Mabel.

Anyhow, there was a precedent. There was evidence that this could work. A ghost could be seen if they needed it enough. And Melodie was a ghost, yes, but she needed to be seen. And she needed to be heard.

The Lady in White *clip-clopped* closer.

Melodie walked slowly and then she quickened, and she stomped, and she hummed, quietly, only to herself. She hummed a marching song, a courage song, and she thought of all the facts she knew about honey badgers, the toughest animals on Earth.

She had read about them in books.

And her father had told her stories about them.

And her mother had said, 'You should make up a song about honey badgers! About how they fight!'

And so Melodie had done just that.

She remembered it.

And, in the middle of the path, Melodie and the lady met.

And at first ...

At first, the lady looked straight through her. As if she wasn't there.

Melodie held her breath.

She wanted to run.

She wanted to turn on her heel and run, all the way back to Direleafe Hall and safety.

Because something about this woman scared her. Something about her eyes. There was a violence about them. She looked past Melodie and up at Direleafe Hall as if she wanted to tear it apart and break it into pieces.

And this was Melodie's home.

And Ms Gallow was weary and melancholy, as if she had forgotten her power.

So, Melodie had to believe in her own power.

And Melodie Rose's power was in song.

'See me.'

It was a tremulous whisper, at first.

'See me.'

And then her voice grew louder.

'See ME!'

And the notes, this time, were pure and loud and resounding, and the stars in the sky began to sing, too, and show off their joy and brightness.

But neither Melodie nor the Lady in White noticed the stars.

They were both too intent on staring at each other.

25
What happened after

Hollowbeak watched from the silver birch tree.

The ghost girls watched, as well, and listened from Melodie's bedroom window.

And, up in her own bedroom, Ines Amontillado looked down, also, on the strange unfolding scene.

Melodie Rose was down there.

Ines Amontillado had watched Melodie Rose, intently, ever since she arrived at Direleafe Hall. She watched, secretly, when Melodie wasn't looking. And down in the depths of her, in the very middle of her heart, Ines wished to be friends with Melodie – this vivid, noisy, shining girl who didn't seem to need anyone but herself.

Ines wished she hadn't failed at the adventure, the invitation, the quest to save Direleafe Hall. Maybe then ...

But Ines always failed no matter how hard she tried, how hard she fought.

She hoped she would have another chance to help Melodie Rose.

In the meantime, she watched. And the ghost girls and Hollowbeak watched, as well, as Melodie stood on her tiptoes, whispered in the Lady in White's ear, and the lady stilled.

They watched as Melodie took a step away and beckoned for the lady to follow.

They watched as both of them disappeared, inside Direleafe Hall.

26
The truth about the Lady in White

The Lady in White looked at Melodie in the flickering candlelight. 'You're not a ghost,' she said. Her eyes narrowed. 'You said outside that you were. And I thought – I didn't believe it, of course – I don't believe in ghosts. But I wondered—'

'I *am*!' Melodie protested. 'How else could I know everything I know about you when you were at school?'

'That I don't know,' the Lady in White said. She spread her hands. 'Perhaps Ms Gallow told you.'

'Did Ms Gallow *know*?' asked Melodie. 'Did

she know it was you who dropped the paint? Did she know how mean you were to Mabel Clattersham, all those years ago? And did she know all the other things?' Melodie listed them, then, all the things that Hollowbeak had told her. All the things that this lady – then a girl – had done.

This lady, *Georgiana.*

Hollowbeak had even told her a thing that Wonder and Mabel had said about this lady, who had been a girl, called *Georgiana Kinch*: she wasn't obvious in her evil; she was like a kitten who hides its claws beneath white velvet fur.

Melodie sat with the Lady in White on the long, narrow wooden bench that stretched down the spine of the damp locker room, and she told Georgiana all the things that Hollowbeak had seen. All the people who Georgiana had broken far worse than these cracked Direleafe walls.

The girl whose glasses Georgiana had

smashed.

The girl who loved books, whose books Georgiana had torn apart.

The girl who loved her, whose heart Georgiana had torn.

So many girls, broken and bruised, and Hollowbeak had seen it all.

At the end of everything, Melodie stared at this lady, Georgiana, and she waited.

After an awfully long time, Georgiana spoke. She said, 'Of course Ms Gallow knew. Why do you think I saved all the money – every scrap I earned in every terrible job – for all those years? Why do you think I lived like a pauper 'til I had enough tucked away to buy this place? Why do you think I want to destroy it?'

'I don't know why at all,' Melodie told her. 'Why do you want to destroy Direleafe Hall?'

The Lady in White clasped her hands in her lap. 'Because,' she said, quietly, 'Ms Gallow told my mother of all the things I'd done. And my mother was so disappointed. She is such a good woman, so kind and so *giving*, and I … I was her opposite. And now every night I dream of it all.' Georgiana whispered, 'I dream of me, back here, doing all those things. I dream of all my misdeeds and how horrible I was, and I can never escape it, and I will never escape it until this place is *gone*. And I am so afraid … I was so afraid …' She shook her head. 'Why am I telling you all this?' Georgiana scowled. 'It's because you're looking at me like that. As if you can see inside of me.'

She stood, sharply, and strode towards the door.

'Wait!' Melodie cried out.

Georgiana paused but did not turn.

'Why?' Melodie asked her. 'Why were you afraid? My friend saw your house – your family. He said they seem happy.'

When Georgiana spoke, it was as though her mouth was filled with glass splinters. 'That's why I was afraid,' she said. 'Because I was *never* happy. No matter what I did. I could never feel it. I could never laugh the way my family did. I could never be ... like them. I hurt people without trying, at first, and then I did it because at least ... that was feeling something. I hurt the girls. I hurt my mother. And she was *so disappointed in me.*'

Georgiana turned to face Melodie again. She inclined her head to one side. 'You look like her,' she whispered. 'Ms Gallow. I hated her. I always knew she saw who I really was. She still looks at me like that. I don't want to be seen like that anymore. I want to be *free*. I ...' Georgiana shook her head. 'I need to go, now,' she muttered.

'Where to?' Melodie blurted. 'Where do you live? Where is your home?'

Georgiana laughed, sharp and joyless. 'I don't have a home,' she said. 'People like me don't have *homes*.' Georgiana narrowed her grey-cloud eyes at Melodie. 'You're not a ghost,' she repeated.

'I am,' said Melodie.

Georgiana reached across the space between them, and she pinched Melodie's skin between her bony fingers.

Melodie cried out in pain. She pushed up her sleeve and looked at her arm. A red shape, almost star-like, blazed on her freckled skin.

'There,' said Georgiana. 'See? You are not a ghost. You're *ordinary*. You have no powers. No powers at all.'

Georgiana strode away, the noise of her footsteps echoing off the floorboards. The echo of her words seemed louder, still.

Melodie stood, alone, in the damp, mouldering room. Her arm burned, but that wasn't the worst of her pain.

It felt as though she'd been cracked in two, torn from the inside out.

She looked at herself in the mirror, expecting to see her body, shattered. Instead, she saw, properly, herself.

So bright-haired.

So bright-eyed.

So tall.

So solid.

So many bones.

Melodie, tentatively, touched the red welt on her arm. And then she touched the place on her brow where the other welt had been, the one from the conker.

Melodie pressed a hand against the mirror glass. She felt the chill of it.

She felt it.

She felt all of it.

She felt the cold of the glass and the warmth in the air. She felt the tightness in her lungs. She felt her heart beating, beating, beating ...

She felt her *heart.*

Tears sprang to her eyes.

She felt her heart.

And she knew. Of course, perhaps, she had always known.

Melodie walked out into the gloom, and she climbed up the silver birch tree and sat beside Hollowbeak.

'I feel my heart,' she said. 'My pulse, my blood. I feel my *blood*, Hollowbeak.'

Hollowbeak peered at her for an awfully long time. He saw the tears on her cheeks, the angry red swelling on her arm. He saw the faint scabbing on her brow. He saw how she glowed like the sun.

He knew, then, the truth of it all. Perhaps he had always known.

You are not a ghost, said Hollowbeak.

'I thought I was,' murmured Melodie. She blinked up at him with shining eyes. 'I thought that was why my mother left me.'

Melodie looked at Hollowbeak. He peered at her, sadly, knowingly.

'If I am alive, then that is not the reason,' whispered Melodie.

Hollowbeak extended a wing. A feather touched her hand.

'I am not a ghost,' whispered Melodie.

Hollowbeak shook his head. *You are not a ghost.*

'Then why hasn't my mother returned?'

Maybe she is sad, said Hollowbeak. *Maybe we are all sad, and this is why we all do these things. But you are not a ghost, Melodie Rose. And do you know what that means?*

Melodie looked into his eyes. 'I can make anyone see me,' she said.

27
Remembering

On the day her father died, the sky was as blue as a fairy-wren's belly.

They walked along the road, Melodie skipping and racing along, clutching her father's hand, dragging him onwards.

Her father seemed quieter that day than he usually was, despite the sunshine.

So Melodie filled the silence with facts and songs. She was loud and she was laughing, and she held his hand so tightly. She loved the feel of it – her skin and his skin, together, always.

She told him all about birds and fish and that anteaters have teeth.

But he was so quiet.

Why was he so quiet?

And then, with no announcement, no fanfare, no warning ...

He fell.

And Melodie fell with him because she never let go of his hand.

And then it was days and nights of tears. Her mother's tears and her own.

And then the final day came. Melodie didn't know, of course, that it was the final day.

She should have known.

★

Storm clouds made a murky lake of the sky.

Melodie's mother got a coat for Melodie, but she didn't get shoes for herself, and they climbed into her rusted Sunbird, with the gashes in the seats where Melodie hid treasures.

And they drove.

Through the potato fields and through the sheep fields and through the tulip fields, and all the way to Direleafe Hall.

And Direleafe Hall was like the castles she'd read about in books – tall and grey and vine-covered. She imagined some hunching beast lurking in there, but one with a very kind heart.

This was a kind place – Melodie could tell.

She followed her mother to the door of Direleafe Hall.

And her mother said to Melodie, 'I know it looks grim and a little bit shattered, but sometimes the best hearts are like that.'

Melodie pressed her small, soft hand to the door of Direleafe Hall, and she was almost sure, then, that she could feel it – a heartbeat. Her mother was right.

'This is your home, now,' her mother said.

'But, what about you?' asked Melodie. 'Where will your home be?'

Her mother's face was wet with tears. 'My home is always with you, my sunrise.'

'Then why—'

'Grief is a thing that can't be fixed,' her mother whispered. 'But sadness can be eased a little.

I need to find a way to ease my sadness.'

'Without me?'

'So I can be better for you. So I can give you a home, with me, again.'

'Here? You said here is my home,' said Melodie.

'Perhaps,' her mother said. 'In the meantime, Melodie, forget about me, for just a little while.' She leaned closer. 'And never stop singing, please. Your songs make the stars shine. Without them, everything is darkness. Now knock, won't you? Go on. Turn and knock.'

And so, Melodie did as she said. She turned and she knocked. Once, twice, three times.

And she turned back to her mother to say, 'Please don't go.'

But her mother was gone. Into the air. Into the clouds. Away.

And she opened her mouth – to sing or to scream – but all that came out was air.

And the world around her was swirling.

And the sky around her was so dark, so dark – there were no stars at all. Not one.

And all Melodie could hear was her mother's command: 'Forget about me, for just a little while.'

And as Melodie collapsed on the steps of Direleafe Hall, that's exactly what she did.

28 Telling the truth about all of it

In the morning, after another sleepless night, Melodie told the ghost girls the truth of it.

'Why can you see us, then,' asked Nell, with a snarl, 'if you're not even dead?'

'It doesn't seem fair,' added Lucy, her chin wavering.

'It's *not* fair,' said Nell, shaking her head. 'I can't believe I ever thought you were special. I can't believe I thought you might save us. All it was, all along, was that you were *not dead*. That was the only thing different about you. You're not special one bit.'

'She is,' Lucy whispered. 'Remember when

she sang—'

'We thought you were one of us,' said Florence, interrupting. She would not meet Melodie's eyes.

'I am one of you,' said Melodie. 'And I'm not. And as to *why* I can see you ... I don't know how to explain it. But ...' Melodie took a deep breath. 'My father died while he held my hand. Hollowbeak says if a person is close to death, or has been, they can *see*, just like a ghost can. I held his hand and I never let go and his skin was my skin and I fell with him and ... well ... I know it sounds strange.'

'It surely does,' grumbled Nell. She glared at Hollowbeak. 'Before her, it was only ghosts who could see us. I don't like it when the rules change. I don't like it when I don't know things.'

'Strange things happen at Direleafe Hall,' said Lucy. 'It's part of its magic.'

Hollowbeak moved in between them, with his funny, bobbing walk. *Whether Melodie is or isn't a ghost won't matter one bit if none of you exist. And you won't if Direleafe is destroyed,* he said.

'Direleafe Hall is your home,' said Melodie. She looked at her friends, beseechingly. 'And it's my home, too, now. I hope you'll forget I'm not a ghost and remember that I am still one of you. We need to help each other. Bad things only happen in this place – and to this place – when girls are not good to each other. When girls *help* each other, that is when they can be truly powerful.'

'Who are you talking to?' said a sharp voice behind them.

Melodie jumped and so did Hollowbeak and so did the three ghost girls.

Melodie turned, slowly. 'You see me?' she whispered. But, of course, she had always known she did.

The girl's brow furrowed. 'Of course, I see you,' she said. And then she asked again, 'Who were you talking to?'

'My friends,' said Melodie because it felt

wrong to say *nobody*. 'But you can't see *them*.'

'Okay,' said the girl, with a shrug. She sat down on Melodie's bed. 'What were you talking about?' she asked.

'Saving Direleafe Hall,' replied Melodie. 'You tried to help me before.'

'I know,' said the girl.

'You knew it was me you were helping?' gasped Melodie.

'Of course,' said the girl. 'I'm sorry I failed. I want another chance, if you'll let me. I want to help.'

Melodie smiled. And then she said, 'You never failed, Ines. I think there was no way of succeeding, that time. But maybe this time there is if we work together.'

Before you agree, whispered Hollowbeak to Melodie, *you need to ask: is she any good at scaring?*

'Did the bird just talk to you?' asked Ines.

She sees me? asked Hollowbeak.

'You see him?' asked Melodie.

Ines nodded.

I don't like it, whispered Hollowbeak, *when the rules change.*

Nell smirked.

'Flimsy science,' Florence muttered.

'Magic,' whispered Lucy.

'He asked if you're good at scaring,' said Melodie. She glared at Hollowbeak. 'Do you promise we won't be too cruel?'

Hollowbeak's button eyes sparkled. *You're in charge,* he replied.

Ines smiled at Hollowbeak and it turned her face to sunshine. 'I,' she replied, with no small amount of pride, 'am most excellent at scaring.'

29
Preparations

To prepare for the scaring, they went hunting for costumes. Two ghost masks were found in the dusty wooden dress-up chest at the back of the school hall. They were greying and mildewed with age but this, somehow, added to their menace.

'I want to wear one!' cried Nell. She held up her hands, shaped into claws.

'I'm sorry, Nell,' said Melodie, cautiously, fearful of Nell's forceful eyes, 'but it's just—'

'Look at you, Miss La-di-da,' she said, her eyebrows downwards-pointing knives. 'You've been one of the living for all of five minutes, and you're already shutting us out.'

'It's not like that,' said Melodie. 'You're seen by the people who matter to you, the people who love you. And I still think I *am* mostly like you three, actually.'

'You're not,' said Florence, crossing her arms. 'If you're not a ghost, then you're not stuck here, at Direleafe Hall, like we are. You're free to go whenever you like.'

'But maybe it's not how you think it is,' Melodie said. 'Maybe you *can* leave, after all. Wonder Quinn left, didn't she?' She turned to Hollowbeak. 'How?' she asked him.

I think, said Hollowbeak, *that she simply found out why she was tethered here – the thing she had to do that would sever the string. And when that thing was done, she could leave.* He said the last part in the saddest voice Melodie had ever heard. And then he flew away.

'So, that's it,' said Melodie. 'That's what you have to do – discover the thing that's tethering you to this place and just ... sever the string.'

The three girls were silent a time before Lucy, timidly, spoke up. 'Perhaps it's this,' she said. 'Perhaps it's protecting Direleafe Hall. Perhaps that's why we're still here. It's our job to save this place.'

'Don't be ridiculous,' said Nell.

At the same time, Melodie smiled at her. 'I think you might be on to something, Lucy,' she said, gently. Her brow knitted. 'But wait, I thought you loved it here. I thought that was why we were saving it.'

'We do,' said Nell, folding her arms. 'Lucy is just being silly, as usual.'

Lucy stared at her feet, her lower lip beginning to tremble.

Nell's lip curled. 'Ridiculous,' she said.

'Anyhow, you're all getting distracted,' said Florence. 'Let's get back to the next point on the list. The *scaring*. Melodie, you said that Ms Gallow told you that the Lady in White is returning tonight? We don't have very much time!'

Melodie nodded, and she tried to smile but she couldn't. She did not tell any of them – because she did not know how – about the feeling she had, deep in her chest, that this scaring idea was not the right way to go about things at all.

She knew she'd agreed to it, but the whole idea just felt ...

As if it lacked humanity.

★

'If anyone is ever unkind, appeal to their humanity. Appeal to the small spark within them that is still made of stardust. That's the purest thing. We are stardust. That's what being human means. If a person is unkind, it's only that they've forgotten. To remind them, show them kindness yourself. Show them joy. If that doesn't work, show them the stars.'

★

Melodie had had enough fear for one lifetime – her father had died, her mother had left.

Direleafe Hall was not a place for fear.

It was a place for love, and for humanity. For the sunrises. For the stars.

Just then, a sparkling thing fell down upon Melodie's palm – a piece of tinsel, perhaps, from some long-ago party or country dance.

'What is it?' said Lucy. 'It looks like stardust.'

'Perhaps it is,' said Melodie. 'Perhaps it fell all the way from the heavens.'

30
Hollowbeak's sadness

Hollowbeak sat on one of the cobwebbed rafters. He caught a large spider in his claw, just because he could. Just because he was sad.

But these girls, they had made it less. Made the pain less sharp. Made it smaller. But it would still be there. It would always be there. The pull and the yearning. The hole in his heart. The hollowness down to the bones of him.

When a person leaves, they do not leave behind them nothing. They leave behind a tear and a gaping hole that can never be fully healed. It can only be stitched, over and over – patched up each time it splits apart.

And a word can split it.

And a memory.

And the only things that can stitch it are love and time.

Hollowbeak held the dead spider in his claws and he let himself utter a single, small, sad *caw*.

And then he flew down to join the girls. They did not replace his Wonder. But they were something. And he did, despite himself, quite love this Melodie Rose.

Even though she had too many bones.

And now she wore a mask like a ghoul. And Ines wore one like a wraith. And behind the two masks were two brave children about to do a scaring. About to make a difference. About to fix things.

About to save Direleafe Hall.

Hopefully.

And their love for the hall and Hollowbeak's love for them made one small stitch across the sadness.

31
The ballad of Melodie Rose

On the gates of Direleafe Hall, there sat five girls in a row.

Two of them could be seen, because they were alive. Three of them could only be seen by one of the girls and one unearthly crow.

Two of the girls wore ghastly masks. Three of them wore only their own faces.

The five girls were united – bonded – by their plan.

One of them – a girl with hair like the sun and a heart even bigger – hummed to herself.

A ballad.

A song which, in her head, was all about

courage and the stars and home.

Eventually she fell silent and she joined the girls in their watching.

They watched the path that approached Direleafe Hall, winding as a slithering snake.

They watched as the Lady in White approached. Her hair was like a helmet, her eyes like steel and midwinter frost, and she wore a mask much more frightening than the ones worn by Melodie and Ines. Four of the girls, as they were meant to, felt fear when they saw her.

Melodie Rose felt only empathy.

Poor Georgiana. Poor her.

It felt unimaginably sad that Georgiana Kinch did not visit her parents, her living brother. That she didn't laugh with them, sing with them, sit with her mother on the front porch, a warm cat on her knee.

It felt unimaginably sad that Georgiana could not visit her old school without feeling repugnance and shame.

Now that her memory had returned, Melodie knew what it was like to be haunted by the past. Memories are like ghosts.

Ines Amontillado knew it, too. For Ines, her pain was now, always, but not so much at Direleafe Hall. *Unless.* Unless she was allowed to continue her small cruelties, long enough that they made her black inside, just like Georgiana Kinch. Ines could still break free from her past. If they saved the one place where she felt at home. Before she became bitter. Or, worse, before she became a ghost.

Georgiana Kinch was *alive.* She should not still be tied to all the pain in her past. She should not be marching up the path to Direleafe Hall with such coldness in her expression, with such precise intent. She should not wish to destroy Direleafe Hall.

Melodie watched as Ines Amontillado readied herself to terrify. She watched as the ghost girls did the same. And she knew more clearly than ever that this plan would fail.

'I have to do something else,' she whispered. 'I have to do something better.'

'Whatever it is,' she heard a voice beside her say, 'whatever it is, you can do it.'

Melodie turned to see Ines beside her.

'I threw a conker at you because I wanted you to see me like I see you. You don't have to throw conkers, Melodie Rose. You glow already. Whatever it is that needs to be done, you can do it.'

Ines took Melodie's hand and she squeezed. 'If it helps,' she said, 'I'll keep holding your hand until it's done.'

'I don't know *how*, yet,' Melodie whispered. 'I don't know how to fix it.' She met Ines's eye. 'I didn't even know you could see me, until a blink ago. I don't even know who I am.'

Ines looked at her fingertips. 'I don't know how to say who you are, Melodie Rose. You are the only one who knows that. But I know what I see. You are Melodie.' She smiled. 'You are a song.'

And then Hollowbeak, who was listening, added, *You are a song, and you are seen and you are heard.*

And the three ghost girls chimed in, then: 'You are a song and you are seen and you are heard and you belong.'

'You are not alone,' Ines finished. 'We will stand beside you. And ...' She pointed up. 'You have the stars. They will help you.'

'Sing to them,' whispered Lucy.

Melodie met her eye. Lucy nodded.

And Melodie felt it.

Yes.

This.

This was right.

She looked at Hollowbeak, who nodded. *Sing, Melodie Rose, and see what happens. See what your song can do.*

'You can do this,' Ines said. 'And I will hold your hand, all the while. I won't ever let go.'

Melodie took off her mask and smiled at Ines. Her heart – that had been so still and silent for so long – was now beating a rhythm inside her that sounded exactly like her song. She listened to its rhythm, *her* rhythm. She opened her mouth, and she did not hum, this time. She *sang* the song of her heart and her soul to the stars.

Her song.

She sang with all her heart.

The Ballad of Melodie Rose.

In the morning, we are born, full of stardust,
Still in a dream cocoon.
And the stars are our mothers and fathers
Who shield us against the gloom.
And we sing a sweet song to the sunrise
And we sing our goodbyes to the moon
We touch the window of our warm, safe home
And the stars whisper, 'We'll see you soon.'
In the dawning, the stars sing a song to us,
And they sing, 'We will watch over you.
We are part of you, you are part of us
And we'll watch as you grow and bloom.

And when you sing us your sweet ballad,
We'll sing our song back down to you.
And we'll give you a home and we'll give you our
love,
And we'll show you humanity, too.
For we are you, and you are us, dear,
And full of our fire are you.
You are never alone, and you are never unseen
For made of our stardust are you.
You are never alone, and you are never unseen
For made of our stardust are you.'

Melodie finished her song and, for a moment, nothing happened. For a moment, the sky remained just as it always had been.

But then, one by one, the stars began to shine a little brighter, a little stronger.

And then, even brighter still, until the sky was as bright as daytime.

And the light of the stars lit up Direleafe Hall so brightly it blazed. Just like it always had inside.

One by one, the pupils came out from the inside of Direleafe Hall. And so did Ms Gallow, holding the hand of Rowan Underhill, who was struggling to be brave. And Ms Gallow's eyes still twinkled, just like the stars, and her mouth opened, and she was, somehow, young again.

She stared at the stars in astonishment. So did the girls on the gate and the black bird circling in the sky.

And so, wonderfully, incredibly, did Georgiana Kinch.

And maybe Melodie made it happen, this miracle of starlight, or maybe it was magic – the magic of Direleafe Hall. In the end, it didn't matter. It mattered that it happened at all and that was the end of that.

As Georgiana Kinch stared upwards, her face ... changed. It opened. It illuminated. Because no human can stare at the stars in their full brilliance and not be changed, in a way.

And while they all gazed in wonder at the

sky, Melodie skidded down from the gate and she moved over to Ms Gallow's side. And Ms Gallow said in a hush, 'Why do I feel like you did this?'

It was at just this moment that through the gates of Direleafe Hall came Georgiana's mother, to whom Hollowbeak had delivered a note, earlier in the afternoon. Georgiana's mother was the sort of person who came when crows delivered mysterious notes.

Georgiana did not see her mother, at first, so entranced was she by the sky.

She did not see her mother until she was right beside her. Until her mother put her hand on her shoulder.

Melodie's whole body tightened, as she watched.

And then ...

And *then* ...

Mrs Kinch opened her arms as wide as the horizon. And Georgiana collapsed into them, her shoulders shaking. And Melodie could almost *see* the weight of everything leaving her, like vapours into the sky.

Ms Gallow said, quietly, 'Something tells me you've fixed everything, my darling Melodie Rose.' And then she moved away to Georgiana and her mother.

Melodie, smiling, looked up, one more time. The clouds were covering the stars, dimming them. Melodie sang her song again, just quietly, and they brightened once more, a little.

Hollowbeak Crow heard the song. He hummed along. And he was ... *happy*.

The three ghost girls leaped down from the gates. And Nell and Florence smiled – joyful that it was done, that Direleafe Hall was safe.

But then, piercing the joy, there came a sword-sharp howl.

32
Lucy's cry

It was Lucy – the quiet one, the shy one – who turned her face to the sky and *roared*.

She stood up. Right there. Right on top of the gate, the iron digging into her feet. She stood, and she screamed at the stars, 'Please! Please, take us! Why did you not take us? Please, will you take us, now?'

'Lucy!' Nell growled. 'Lucy, stop that at once.'

Lucy turned to face her, her expression incendiary. 'I will *not*!' she said. 'I will not stop.'

'But this is what we wanted,' said Florence. 'This is our home.'

'It *has* been our home,' said Lucy. 'And it is

my dearest home, but I want ... I want ...' She shook her head, her curls bouncing. 'I want to see them, Florence! I want to see the *stars*! We have been here for so long, and every person we have loved has gone away to something else. All the girls and all the schoolmistresses and that boy with the feathers for hair. And it was *those people* who made this our home. Everyone who left made it less so, and I have *forgotten* most of them, Nell. I have forgotten most of the girls, and I think it is because my heart is almost gone entirely. And, one day soon, Ms Gallow will go, and Melodie will go, in her time, and I don't want to *still be here*. I thought ... I thought if we helped with this saving of Direleafe Hall, maybe ... maybe we would go as well.'

'That was never the intention,' said Nell. 'That was never the plan.'

'No,' whispered Lucy. 'But perhaps it was the hope. Or, at least, I think it secretly was for me.' She met Nell's eye. 'And I'm not ridiculous,' she said, bravely.

Nell stared at Lucy for a long, heavy time. And Florence did, as well.

Finally, Florence spoke. 'I think I want to go, too. There is so much else to discover, isn't there? Imagine what a person might discover in the stars.'

Nell looked between them, astounded. But then she shrugged, and she said, 'Well, I'm not going to let you two go and leave me behind. You'll be useless without me. How do we make it happen, though?'

'Perhaps,' said Lucy, quietly, 'we just hold hands and we stand beside each other and, together, we hope. And perhaps ...' She smiled shyly at Melodie. 'Our friend Melodie Rose might sing the stars her song again.'

'Lucy,' said Melodie, quietly, 'I think we should have listened to you more often. And ...' She did not want to say it; she did not *want* them to leave, but she knew how much they wanted it. 'Of course, I will sing you my song.'

The three ghost girls exchanged a look, *exhilarated*, and then each of them reached out and took the hand of another one. And it felt, to Melodie, as if this act were the most powerful act of all.

And Melodie began to sing again.

It happened slowly, this time – a star here and there, nervously showing itself. Then, other stars, buoyed by the courage of their companions, began to show off their magnificence, too. One by one, they made spotlights of themselves, until the sky was lit up like day.

Ines and Melodie looked up, squinting.

'Well,' whispered Lucy, still standing, glowing against the sky like a hero carved in marble. 'This is a thing.'

'It is,' said Nell. She glared at Lucy. 'It's your fault if it's horrible up there.'

Florence smiled at both of them. 'It won't be. It will be an adventure.'

A song flew down from the heavens, then.

A ballad that was for only the three ghost girls.

My small, precious hatchlings,
In your nest, tucked in tight,
Flutter down your eyelids
And fly to me tonight ...

'Is this goodbye?' Melodie asked, as the girls began to ... Melodie did not know what to call it. Did they fade? Did they shimmer? Were they made into silvery angels?

Whatever it was, it was beautiful and so incredibly sad.

'You said you'd always be here,' she whispered. 'I thought you'd never leave.'

Nell gave her a rare, beautiful smile. 'We won't ever leave you, really. We'll just be up there.' She pointed.

'I don't want to say goodbye,' Melodie said. 'You are my friends.'

'You'll be with us one day,' said Lucy.

'Thank you,' said Florence. 'You were a good friend. And, look, now you can say you are friends with the stars.'

Then the sky got brighter still, so bright that Melodie closed her eyes. And there came a sound, like an exhalation, like a *letting go*.

When Melodie opened her eyes again ...

There was a gleaming where the three girls had been, a sort of imprint of them in the sky. As Melodie watched, ever so slowly the gleaming faded.

Nell, Florence and Lucy had gone to the stars.

Just then, a hand squeezed hers, small and warm. 'Don't be sad. We have each other,' said Ines, as Melodie wiped at her tears. And then Ines said to Melodie, 'Direleafe Hall was never going to be fixed with fear. Fear never fixes anything.'

Melodie smiled, small and sad. 'True,' she said. 'Instead, Direleafe Hall was saved by ...'

'It was saved by *us*,' Ines said, definitively.

'It was saved by us Direleafe girls. Working together.'

And a crow, said Hollowbeak, landing between them.

'Yes,' said Ines, replying to him. 'And you, too, Hollowbeak.'

You hear me? whispered Hollowbeak. *Only ghosts could see me, before. Only ghosts could hear me.*

'Things are changing,' said Melodie Rose. 'Perhaps *you* are changing. Perhaps you are becoming more alive.'

Flimsy science, said Hollowbeak.

33
And then …

In the days that came after, the two girls who stayed talked at length about what had happened that night.

They knew it was a kind of magic.

Ines told Melodie that she wished she had done more to help (she *was* most excellent at scaring, after all).

Melodie assured Ines that just being there was enough, that her friendship was enough, that being beside her and holding her hand – sometimes, that's all a person needs.

Ines had seemed to glow, then, when Melodie talked of friendship.

Sometimes, while Melodie and Ines sat together, talking and laughing, they were joined by a small, timid girl who reminded Melodie of Lucy. Rowan Underhill had always wanted to be Melodie's friend as well, secretly, quietly. And so now Melodie had two friends – three if you counted Hollowbeak.

But Melodie and Ines were bonded, closer than they could be bonded to any other girl. They were becoming something like best friends. They had something in common, after all – Direleafe Hall was the only place where they belonged.

In the days that came after, Georgiana Kinch and Ms Gallow talked constantly. Georgiana agreed to halt the sale of Direleafe Hall and to use some of her money to help with repairs to the building.

They talked about trying to recruit more girls, but both decided that the girls who were there were enough. Others would find their way to Direleafe Hall, in their own time, if they needed it.

Somehow, girls who needed it always found their way to Direleafe Hall.

Or back to it.

And Ms Gallow and Georgiana became proper friends.

Neither of the women had had a friend – a proper friend – in so long that the memory of it had faded, had turned into cobwebs and dust.

A friend.

Now. That was a thing.

Sometimes, at night-time, Georgiana sat with her mother on the front porch and they listened to old records together.

They didn't say much to each other. They held hands. That was enough.

In the days that came after, a woman with bare feet put on her shoes again.

She climbed into her Sunbird car and she turned on the engine.

She took a deep breath and, as the car pulled away and onto the road, towards the rising sun, she began to sing. It was a song her daughter had sung her once, about honey badgers.

She hoped it would give her courage.

She hoped her daughter would forgive her. She hoped her daughter would understand that her heart had been broken and she had been so filled up with sadness there had been no room for anything else, even a girl as shining as Melodie Rose.

She couldn't wait to see her daughter again.

She couldn't wait to hear her sing.

Epilogue

Hollowbeak sat on the roof of Direleafe Hall. On his left side, there sat Ines Amontillado. On his right side, there sat Melodie Rose (who might be his best friend – though he'd never admit it).

And all that was beneath him, a little bit cracked, a little bit broken, but *still here*, was Direleafe.

Hollowbeak Crow belonged at Direleafe Hall.

He was *alive* here.

And Melodie was alive.

And Ines was alive.

And Ms Gallow was alive.

This place was alive.

The girls and women within it were full of vibrant, beautiful, bewildering life, and full of hope, too.

And wonder.

And Hollowbeak Crow felt it all, for the first time in such a long time. He felt the *aliveness* of this place. He felt the magic of it.

Hollowbeak Crow had always been at Direleafe Hall. And he would be here until forever.

Because Melodie still needed him.

Because she had asked him to stay.

And Hollowbeak had grunted, grouchily, and shook his shiny black head.

But he was secretly happy. Happy to stay. Happy to be with Melodie – who was too loud and too much and too *alive* – but was also his friend.

As long as she needed him, he would stay.

As long as Direleafe Hall needed him, he would stay.

This crow no longer wished to go to the stars.

He liked it well enough here, on the roof of Direleafe Hall. He liked it well enough with these girls.

Because he saw, now, it was not only Wonder. It had *never* been only Wonder. There had been girls before her. There would be more girls who he could help. They would find their way here when they needed to.

It was nice to help.

It was nice to be *needed.*

Maybe that's why you see me, he said to Melodie Rose. *You and Ines. It's not because you are a ghost. Maybe it's because you need me.*

'Or maybe,' said Melodie Rose, light as a feather, 'it's because you need us.'

Hollowbeak peered at Melodie. And he thought, then, of Wonder. And he thought of the girl in the tulip field.

He thought of how Melodie was too loud, too bright, too *humming*, and she was not a ghost.

He thought of how Wonder was made of heart and longing.

He thought of how the girl in the tulip field, all those years ago, was mean and wild and wicked and strong.

And he thought that Melodie might be right.

'Maybe you need us and this place,' said Melodie. 'Maybe you have always been here. Maybe you will always be here. Maybe you are the one who will stay here forever, not because you are tied here but because you *choose* to stay, your claws curled around the heart of this place. Maybe that's just the way it is.'

Hollowbeak didn't know what to say, and Melodie didn't wait for him to say anything. Instead, Melodie sang again. She sang often, these days. Loudly.

Hollowbeak pretended he didn't like it.

But he did.

After she had finished her singing, she sighed, contentedly. The music of the lullaby grew fainter. And then it was gone.

The two girls leaned their small heads together and Hollowbeak sat beside them.

And they were happy.

And Melodie tore up the two pieces of paper that she had kept in her pocket. One was a list of how to save Direleafe Hall, and one was the note that had been pinned to her chest.

She tore them and she let the wind take them. Because now was not a time for lists or notes that said *goodbye*. Now was a time for love.

And Hollowbeak thought, *I love you.*

And then Hollowbeak thought about love and how love is, when it comes down to it, mostly about being seen and heard. And Hollowbeak saw Melodie now. He saw all the way down to the bones of her. And she saw him.

Hollowbeak cleared his throat. *Tell me, Melodie,* he said. *Tell me some facts about stars.*

Melodie smiled and she did as he said. She told him forty-eight facts about stars and then thirteen about crows. And she knew, all the while that she was telling him, that this was a kind of love. This was Hollowbeak's kind of love.

And the stars shone brightly above them.

And Melodie knew she was alive.

Acknowledgements

This is a book built on gratitude.

I don't have the words to express how much I value and love the team at UQP. Ben, Madonna and Aviva, thank you so much for making UQP the brilliant, adventurous, creative, daring publishing house it is – I am so proud to be one of your authors.

Kristina, who saw something in *Wonder Quinn* and took a chance on it, allowing Melodie to live.

Clair, who is like this wise person, while also being the kindest, gentlest, most perfect ray of sunshine.

Cathy, who somehow knows all the answers and all the right things to say and is understanding and patient far beyond what she should be. And is a complete genius, too.

Kristy, you took this book from a jumble of words and crafted it into something that sang. Thank you. *Thank you*. Editors are actual heroes.

Jean, who fights in my corner tirelessly and makes me smile constantly. And Kate, Denise, Sally and Debbie, who are so good at their jobs, so generous, and don't call me out on my scattiness and neurosis, when they really should.

Rachel ... oh, my stars, what do you say to an artist who literally turns the characters you made up in your head into real, actual people? Rachel, you know I am your biggest fan. I will love you forever for what you have done for this series.

My agent, Brian – you have been so good and gentle and wise and strong and bewilderingly patient with me for so many years now. I literally do not know what I'd do without you.

My #auswrites and #teamsuperfans mates, you know you are my ride-or-dies. I would not ever have persevered without you. I love you more than chocolate.

The reviewers who found *Wonder Quinn* and championed it – how can I ever repay you?

I have a gratitude bigger than the stars for the friends and family who unwaveringly support me through all of this. My dad, his Leigh, my nan – love you all unimaginable amounts. My Leigh. I'd be a stranger in a strange land without you. My brother, Richard. Having you in my life makes everything worthwhile. Thank you for just being here. You make me so happy. I am so proud of you.

Finally, my Tessa Tiger, my walking heart. Thank you for all the hugs, all the smiles and all the laughs. Love you to the moon and back. For real life. Wherever you are, I'm home (and I'll get you a dog soon, I promise).

Kate Gordon grew up in a small town by the sea in Tasmania. She is the author of six novels for teenagers, as well as the picture book *Bird on a Wire*, and the junior fiction series Juno Jones. She now writes middle-grade fiction. *The Heartsong of Wonder Quinn* was published by UQP, in 2020.

Kate was longlisted in the 2019 and 2020 CBCA Book of the Year Awards and received the 2016 IBBY Australia Ena Noël Award. In 2018, she was shortlisted in the Dorothy Hewett Awards for an Unpublished Manuscript, and was commended in the 2018 Vogel's Literary Awards. Her books have been published internationally.

When not writing, Kate reads, listens to Josh Ritter, has grand adventures with her daughter, and tries to ride a bike.

First published 2021 by University of Queensland Press
PO Box 6042, St Lucia, Queensland 4067 Australia

uqp.com.au
reception@uqp.com.au

Cover design and illustration by Rachel Tribout
Internal illustrations by Rachel Tribout
Author photograph by Stephen Lovell
Typeset in 13/20 pt Adobe Text Pro by Post Pre-press Group, Brisbane
Printed in Australia by McPherson's Printing Group

Australian Government | Australia Council for the Arts

University of Queensland Press is assisted by the Australian Government through the Australia Council, its arts funding and advisory body.

A catalogue record for this book is available from the National Library of Australia.

ISBN 978 0 7022 6321 7 (pbk)
ISBN 978 0 7022 6497 9 (epdf)
ISBN 978 0 7022 6498 6 (epub)
ISBN 978 0 7022 6499 3 (kindle)

University of Queensland Press uses papers that are natural, renewable and recyclable products made from wood grown in well-managed forests and other controlled sources. The logging and manufacturing processes conform to the environmental regulations of the country of origin.

MIX
Paper from responsible sources
FSC® C001695
FSC www.fsc.org